A modern re-telling of Little Women

Becoming Jo

Scholastic Children's Books
An imprint of Scholastic Ltd
Euston House, 24 Eversholt Street, London, NW1 1DB, UK
Registered office: Westfield Road, Southam, Warwickshire, CV47 0RA
SCHOLASTIC and associated logos are trademarks and/or
registered trademarks of Scholastic Inc.

First published in the UK by Scholastic Ltd, 2019

Text copyright © Rosefire Ltd, 2019
Cover illustration copyright © David Wardle, 2019

The right of Sophie McKenzie to be identified as
the author of this work has been asserted.

ISBN 978 1407 18815 7

A CIP catalogue record for this book
is available from the British Library.

All rights reserved.
This book is sold subject to the condition that it shall not,
by way of trade or otherwise, be lent, hired out or otherwise circulated
in any form of binding or cover other than that in which it is published.
No part of this publication may be reproduced, stored in a retrieval
system, or transmitted in any form or by any means (electronic,
mechanical, photocopying, recording or otherwise) without prior
written permission of Scholastic Limited.

Typeset in Berkeley by M Rules
Printed by CPI Group (UK) Ltd, Croydon, CR0 4YY

Papers used by Scholastic Children's Books are made
from wood grown in sustainable forests.

1 3 5 7 9 10 8 6 4 2

This is a work of fiction. Names, characters, places,
incidents and dialogues are products of the author's
imagination or are used fictitiously. Any
resemblance to actual people, living or dead,
events or locales is entirely coincidental.

www.scholastic.co.uk

A modern re-telling of Little Women

Becoming Jo

SCHOLASTIC

SOPHIE McKENZIE

For Meg, a true friend.

Part One

Winter

Chapter 1

The central heating isn't working so we've gathered around the fan heater in the living room. The window is frosted from the cold and the skies outside are heavy and dark, like the headaches I get sometimes when I've been writing for too long.

We're talking gifts.

Or, rather, the lack of them.

"Christmas won't be Christmas without any presents," I grumble from our faded armchair.

"I know," groans Meg. She's sitting on the sofa opposite. Both the sofa and the armchair came from our old house but are really too big for this room, which is cluttered with a bookcase at one end (Mum sold the one that matched it), a TV in the corner and a long coffee table in front of the sofa. "There's a Celine knock-off on Asos, and a maxi dress that would be sooo perfect for me. But it's fifty quid more than Mum said we could spend."

I shrug. Trust Meg to be thinking about clothes. She loves poring over celebrity pictures, studying their style. I don't get it myself. Though I'd never say it directly to Meg, I kind of think the whole world of designer products is a bit of a waste of time. It's like this house we're living in – I know Meg and Amy hate how the kitchen table is chipped and the sofa is shabby and the chairs and the carpet are threadbare, but to me it seems comfortable enough, if a bit small.

"Are you sure that dress would really work on you, Meg?" Amy asks, one eyebrow raised. She's perched on the sofa too, one foot dangling over the end, her pink-cased phone in her hand. "I mean . . . you know, maxi dresses can be a bit, er, swamping unless you've got quite long legs. . ."

"Shut up!" Meg and I speak together, rolling our eyes in unison. However different my older sister and I are, there's one thing we definitely have in common, and that's how epically annoying we sometimes find our youngest sister. Amy might be the baby of the family, but she's got a sharper tongue than the rest of us put together, not to mention nuclear levels of self-absorption.

She's also – and I know this gets to Meg a *lot* – extremely pretty. So's Meg, as far as I'm concerned. They've got the same kind of looks, in fact – fine blonde hair, rosy cheeks and big blue eyes – but whereas Meg worries about being short and dumpy and moans that she has a "splodge of a face", Amy's features are delicate and her face is heart-shaped like a pixie's.

And me? Well, I'm dark-haired and tall and skinny, with large hands and a tendency to clumsiness. Nothing like Meg and Amy and not much in the looks department either, though I do have long, shiny hair which Mum says I'll be grateful for one day. Luckily, not being pretty doesn't bother me at all, though I do wish I owned at least one piece of clothing that didn't have a food stain on it.

"Going back to presents," Amy says, giving me and Meg a typically haughty look. "As an artist it's really important I have access to the best tools available. Like Photoshop Lightroom."

I snort. Loudly.

Amy casts a withering glance in my direction. She sticks out her chin. "You just wish you had my talent. And my artistic senile-bilities."

"Your *what?*" Meg asks.

"She means *sensi*-bilities." I laugh.

Meg stiffens. She hates my laugh. Says it's too big, too hearty.

"*Jo*. You sound like a man."

"Looks like one too," mutters Amy.

I suck in my breath. "Better than looking like—"

"I'd just like Daddy to come home," Beth says. We all stop and look at her. "For Christmas," she explains. "I'd just like Daddy to be here."

She's cross-legged on the floor beside my armchair, busy with her knitting. I'd half-forgotten she was in the room. This happens a lot to Beth. She's actually thirteen and three-quarters, over a year older than Amy, but she seems much younger somehow. I wish she would toughen up. Not because I don't love her just as she is, but for her own sake. She's so shy, a lot of the time it's like she's invisible.

"I know," Meg says gently. "But Dad's tour doesn't end for months."

Silence falls as an icy rain drives against the window. We've only been here in this little three-bedroom brick house for a couple of weeks and so far it's rained every day. We're on the outskirts of a town called Ringstone, near the south coast of

England. We had to move from our bigger house nearer London because Mum lost her job as a social worker and Dad's money wasn't enough to cover the rent. He's a humanist – that's a non-religious – minister embedded with British troops in Syria. He's been away for nearly a year now. We speak on Skype whenever we can, but the lag is always terrible and it's hard to know what to say. Mum doesn't like us to tell him anything negative, which I get, but it does means the conversation can get a bit awkward as we stop ourselves mentioning all the bad stuff that's happened recently: the move and the weather and the fact that Amy's so annoying, for instance.

"I wonder what Dad will do on Christmas Day," Beth says.

"Do you think the soldiers give each other presents?" Amy asks.

I open my mouth to tell her that I'm certain the army hands out shiny wrapping paper and pink ribbons for this very purpose. Then I catch sight of Beth's face and press my lips together.

"I'm afraid there's nothing we can do for Dad at Christmas except hope that he's OK," Meg says, and she sounds so sad that a lump rises in my throat.

"Actually, there is one thing we could do," Beth

ventures. "Something he asked us to do while he was away."

I swallow down the lump in my throat. "What's that?"

"He said we should look after Mum," Beth says softly.

"Which we do," Amy says. "Duh, Beth."

I shoot her an exasperated look, then turn to Beth. "Go on. What do you have in mind?"

"Well. . ." Beth glances round, her expression timid but her eyes shiny with hope. "I was thinking maybe instead of dividing Mum's Christmas budget between the four us, perhaps we could pool it and buy something really nice for her instead?"

I'll be honest. My first thought is that I don't want to give up my own present. I've been saving up for ages for a new laptop, and I was hoping my share of the Christmas money would finally mean I could buy one. I want to be a writer. I write every day: homework obviously, when I have to, but also poems and, for the past few months, I've been working on a story which basically started out as a fan-fiction piece inspired by my favourite set of books – Rowena Riddell's *Blacktower* series – and has now taken on a life of its own. Having a new laptop for myself, instead of the ancient one of Dad's with the sticky *r* key, would make all the difference.

But then I think about Mum, and the year she's had: losing her job and having to move without Dad being around to help and worrying all the time about how he is and about money. . . Beth is right: we should give her a nice Christmas after all that stress.

Plus it's clear from Amy's frown that she *totally* hates the prospect of not getting a gift herself. And that's enough to swing it for me.

"Awesome," I say. "Mum deserves it."

"Yes," Meg says, with just a touch of hesitation in her voice. "Yes, Mum would really appreciate that and I can't afford that Asos dress anyway."

"Amy?" Beth asks.

We all look at our youngest sister. She purses her lips and shrugs. I grin. At least Amy knows when she's beaten.

"So what shall we get her?" I ask. "Some books? She loves reading and she never gets the chance these days."

"I was thinking a nice scarf," Meg muses. "Maybe blue, like her eyes."

"No," Amy says. "It's got to be perfume. She

finished that bottle of Acqua di Parma that Aunt Em got her months ago."

"What about a cashmere dressing gown?" Beth suggests. "Mum said she loved the one on the Aspen's website *and* it's reduced right now. If we put all our money together we can easily afford it."

Which is so obviously the best idea that within half a minute it is decided. Meg goes online straightaway to make it happen, while Amy tries to look pleased and Beth beams with delight.

"This gives me an idea for a new scene for my Rachel and Rodriguo story," I say, leaping to my feet and sending the cushion on my lap skidding across the floor, narrowly missing Beth's mint tea. "Let's try it out."

"I'm not being the dog again," Amy mutters, bending over her phone.

"Ooh, Jo, what's it about?" Beth asks. "Is it a Rachel scene? Or a Rodriguo?"

"A Rodriguo, and it's about Christmas," I explain.

I'm writing a love story about a young couple who are being kept apart by the girl's cruel father. Rachel has been sent away to a glamorous but super-strict boarding school, while Rodriguo is travelling the length and breadth of the land trying to find her. I sometimes get my sisters to act out scenes which may or may not make it into the finished novel. Mostly they don't work out – Amy, in particular, is very hard to direct, although I can't fault her for commitment to her part – but on a couple of occasions acting out an idea has given me inspiration for an entire chapter.

I clear my throat, eager to explain what I have in mind: "After many delays and setbacks, Rodriguo is getting close to Rachel's boarding school. It's snowing and bitterly cold and he reckons he's going to arrive just in time for Christmas. On the way he meets a peddler who gives him a bowl of soup because he's starving and the peddler's selling jewellery, so Rodriguo buys a beautiful necklace that he's going to give Rachel when he rescues her. He sets off into the woods near the school. All the trees are covered in snow. Night falls and he is so close, but then. . ." I pause for effect. "But then he hears footsteps – and realizes he's being followed. . ."

Beth shivers. Amy is still staring at her phone, feigning disinterest, but I can tell she's listening.

"Rodriguo is afraid, but he is determined to save Rachel. He keeps going – and just then, out of the darkness. . ." I pause again. Amy looks up, despite herself. "A man with mean, hard eyes appears from behind a tree. He has a monkey with him, a poor, thin, half-starved thing on a chain. He demands money from Rodriguo, who refuses. But. . ."

"Bags be Rodriguo," Meg says. "You always play him, Jo, and it's not fair."

"Fine." I nod impatiently, eager to finish my explanation.

"Who can *I* play?" Amy whines. "And I don't want to be a man or an animal."

"What happens to the monkey, Jo?" Beth asks anxiously.

"Listen." I hold up my hands to quieten them. "Rodriguo gives the man some money but tells him to take the monkey off the chain. He does what Rodriguo asks, then he leaves, but when Rodriguo checks his pocket he finds out the man has stolen the necklace."

Beth's hand flies to her mouth. "Oh no."

"So, what, does Rodriguo take Rachel the mangy old monkey instead?" Amy asks, wrinkling her nose.

"No," I say. "The monkey runs off too."

"Oh, that's sad," Beth says with feeling. "I hope he'll be all right what with all the snow."

"So now Rodriguo is late for Rachel because he stopped to help out a stupid monkey and still doesn't have a present for her," Meg says.

"Exactly." I smile round at them. "I think it's going to be a good one."

"You still haven't said who I can play," Amy points out.

"You can be the peddler who sells Rodriguo the necklace," I say impatiently. "You're very stylish and make this amazing designer jewellery."

Amy says nothing but she's put her phone down.

"I'll be the thief in the forest," I go on. "And Beth can be the monkey."

"Good." Beth sounds relieved. "No lines to remember."

We set up quickly, moving the sofa so that Amy can lay out a tray of rings and necklaces made up of our various bits and pieces of jewellery along the back of it, and Meg, as Rodriguo, can stand on the other side.

I set my phone to record us as Meg mimes taking a bowl of soup from the peddler, then looks down at the tray.

"I'm looking for a necklace," she says in a deep voice. "For the love of my life."

"I have many lovely jewelleries," Amy says, in a flawless cut-glass accent.

"Oh wait." She holds up her hand and turns to

me. "How come Rodriguo can afford one of my necklaces? I thought he didn't have any money?"

"He's going to charm you into giving him a good price," I say, rolling my eyes as I reset my phone. "And don't say 'jewelleries', say 'pieces'."

We start again and eventually, after half an hour of arguing, giggling and several debates about whether the monkey should be limping or not, the scene is in the bag. I watch it back, grinning. It's only barely audible, but there's something there – and it's totally inspired me to go and write a chapter of my story on my laptop.

I bound upstairs to get it all down.

Perhaps it won't be such a terrible Christmas after all.

Chapter 2

Christmas Day and the central heating is working again, thank goodness, so even though there's frost on the window panes and its icy outside, the five of us are snug and warm sitting around the kitchen table. We've had some toast – Mum always makes us eat breakfast before presents – with hot chocolate as a treat, and Mum has just opened her cashmere dressing gown, which she loves.

Aunt Em, who is a major dragon and is thankfully spending the day with friends, is often really generous and has given Mum money for each of us. Mum is planning to use her own share to buy a set of new towels for the bathroom. Ours have worn patches and, in some cases, holes.

"But, Mum," Meg protests. "You should get something for yourself."

"Like perfume," Amy suggests.

"Or books." I cast my youngest sister an irritated glance. It's so obvious Mum isn't bothered about having perfume – that Amy is only thinking about herself, as usual, and hoping to borrow it. But Mum loves reading, especially detective stories. When Dad's home on leave that's what they like doing best – curling up on the sofa with a book each. I haven't seen Mum sit down with a book since we moved.

"I know you all mean well . . ." Mum looks around the table. There are bags under her eyes and a sprinkling of grey hairs that I'm sure weren't there before we moved. She's smiling, but it's impossible to miss how strained her expression is. ". . . but you've already given me my beautiful robe and I'll feel so much better replacing our old towels than getting anything more for myself."

It's true that the towels are pretty shabby. I don't care about stuff like that, of course, but Meg and Amy have moaned about them several times. Not Beth, though. She never complains about anything.

Mum goes on. "Now listen, my loves – I'm afraid we're not going to be able to Skype Dad today."

"What?" My heart sinks. I've been looking forward to talking to Dad all week.

"Oh no," chorus the others.

"Come on," Mum says. She hugs her soft cream cardigan around her chest. It's hanging off her, I suddenly realize, like she's recently lost loads of weight. "No sad faces. There's just no connection where he is right now."

"I'm sure he's thinking of us," Beth says stoutly.

"'Course he is," I agree. Selfishly, I'm now thinking that this will give me more time to work on my book. Writing it is basically my life. The little counter at the bottom of my page says I've written almost twenty-five thousand words, which I save to the cloud every day. I am obsessed with this story. The characters feel as real to me as my own family.

A small hand creeps into mine. It's Beth. I feel guilty – she lives for those calls with Dad. "I suppose I could carry on knitting my scarf," she murmurs.

"And I could paint," agrees Amy.

"What do *you* want to do today, Mum?" Meg asks.

Mum looks round at us. People often say she and I look alike just because we're both tall and slim. I don't see it myself. Her colouring is fair, like Meg and Amy's, and though she's strict as anything when it comes to homework and bedtimes and eating vegetables, there's a softness in her eyes, which are hazel, like Beth's – a softness which I definitely don't share.

"Well," she hesitates. "There *was* something I wanted to suggest to you girls. The local Refuge Now charity is doing a Christmas lunch for some Middle Eastern refugees that have been put up in a hostel down the road. It's shameful the way they have to live." Mum's eyes glint with anger. "They have absolutely nothing, surviving on handouts because they're not allowed to work yet, and they're trying to learn English and make their way . . . and it's up to us to help in whatever way we can."

I nod. I can't imagine what it must be like to have fled your own country yet not be able to make a proper home in another.

"Help how?" Meg asks, always practical.

"Well, several of the refugees are children not much older than you, and lots of them have lost their parents," Mum goes on.

"Oh, that's so sad," Beth breathes, hanging on Mum's every word, her eyes huge. "Those poor people."

"I was thinking," said Mum, looking at each of us in turn, "that we might go along later today and help with their Christmas party."

"What would we have to do?" Amy asks suspiciously.

"Whatever needs doing," Mum says. "Serving, clearing, chatting to the people who come. Try and cheer them up a bit."

"We can do that," I say.

I'm thinking that it will be nice to help the refugee children, but also that maybe I'll get some material for my Rachel and Rodriguo story. I've written about Rodriguo's encounter with the robber and the monkey in the wood, and I'm a bit stuck trying to decide what disaster should next befall him in his quest to rescue tall, skinny, clumsy Rachel from her horrible, oppressive boarding school. So far he's survived a deliberate attempt to run him over, being shot at by a hitman and almost suffocating in a freak earthquake.

"I'm going to put on my red top, then," Meg announces, sweeping out of the room. "It's the most cheering-up thing that I own."

"I want to help, but I don't know if I'll be able to talk to anyone," Beth says, her lips quivering slightly as she sets down her knitting.

"You can just sit with me while I do it then," I say, giving her a wink. "If the point is to cheer up some unhappy people, then you'll be able to do that without trying."

Beth smiles gratefully at me.

"Though if that's the criteria, maybe Amy should stay at home," I can't resist going on.

"Jo," Mum says with a weary shake of her head.

"Hilarious," Amy snaps, and then her hand suddenly flies to her face. "But, oh, suppose they look at my nose?"

I roll my eyes. Amy is obsessed with a tiny bump on her nose that she claims disfigures her entire face.

"Then they'll look," I say impatiently.

"There's nothing wrong with your nose, Amy," Mum adds, concealing a smile.

"There really isn't," Beth insists.

"There is," Amy pouts. "It's Jo's fault for dropping me when I was a baby."

I let out an exaggerated sigh. The story of how I picked Amy up on my fifth birthday – and how she promptly slid out of my hands and landed on the floor – is part of our family folklore.

"Girls!" Mum's voice holds a warning note. She hardly ever loses he temper, but we all know not to push her. "Not today. Today, let's try and be kind."

*

The hostel dining hall is hot and heaving. The scent of roasted vegetables and the sound of earnest chatter and clanking cutlery fills the air. Mum spots Mrs Gardiner, the chairwoman of the Refuge Now charity, and hurries over, leaving the four of us huddled in the doorway. It's a bit overwhelming to be honest. None of us have a clue what to do.

I look around the room. Everyone here is seated, either talking to their neighbour or bent over their food, eating hungrily. Mum's right that there are a lot of young people here. Mostly boys about my age and Meg's. They're dressed in old, ill-fitting jeans and oversized jumpers that must be second-hand – they look like they belong on middle-aged men.

One of the boys wanders over and starts talking to Meg. He's handsome, with caramel skin and soft, floppy dark hair. Meg blushes and smiles. Ugh, how irritating. I can't bear it when she gets like that. Beth shrinks closer to me. Amy juts out her chin. Mostly, the people here are glancing over, then turning back to their dinners and chatting.

Mum bustles over, the charity chairwoman in tow. Mrs Gardiner looks harassed, the powder on her face patchy under a gleam of sweat.

"Thanks for coming, girls," she says. "There's a

table for the younger people in the far corner. Perhaps Abdul can show you?" Mrs Gardiner asks, gesturing at the boy talking to Meg. "While I have a quick chat with your mum."

"Sure," Abdul says, with a grin.

Mum glances at me, then at Beth, and I give her a reassuring nod to show that I'll make sure Beth's OK. Even so, as Mrs Gardiner whisks Mum away and the rest of us troop after Abdul, I'm sure my own heart is beating as hard as Beth's.

There are nine or ten boys and a couple of girls at the "younger people" table. Abdul sits down, ushering Meg into the chair next to him.

Beth is blushing furiously while Amy's chin is stuck firmly in the air, a sure sign that she's also feeling awkward. I take a deep breath and grab Beth's hand.

"Come on," I say, "it's going to be fine." We walk towards the empty seats. Nobody gives us a second glance. Across the room I notice a rickety old piano.

"D'you fancy playing something, Beth?" I ask with a grin. Beth loves the piano, though she hates playing in public. We've never been able to afford our own instrument, but Beth took regular lessons at our old school and the teachers let her practise there whenever she wanted. They said she had real talent.

Beth gazes up at me, horrified. "No," she gasps.

"Are you sure," I tease. "It's a real piano." Since we moved, poor Beth has had to make do with our ancient, second-hand keyboard.

Beth shakes her head furiously, clearly too overawed by the situation to speak. As we reach the chairs a girl who looks about sixteen, the same age as Meg, drifts over. She's elegant with dangling earrings, a long flowing dress and the saddest eyes I've ever seen.

"Hi," she says. "I'm Samira." She sits down between me and Beth and we start talking. Her English is amazing considering she has been in this country for less than two months. She tells us how she's here with her mother and father but they've been separated from her two brothers, and her parents are going mad with worry not knowing where they are.

"That's awful," Beth says, wide-eyed, clearly forgetting her shyness for the moment in characteristic sympathy. "I know it's not the same – but we don't know where our dad is most of the time and I can't stop worrying."

While she and Samira chat away, Amy wanders

off. I see her a few minutes later, talking to some girls her own age. I grin. Trust Amy. She always lands on her feet. Meg calls me over and I sit down next to her. Abdul leans across.

"My friend Lateef wanted to meet you." He points to the boy sitting opposite.

I give him a thoughtful look. He's clearly younger than Abdul, I'm guessing about my own age, with bright, cheerful dark eyes and a cheeky grin.

I like him immediately.

"Hi, I'm Jo," I say. "Jo March."

"You're a writer?" he asks. Unlike Samira and Abdul, he has no trace of an accent.

I glance at Meg, who gives a tiny shrug.

"Well, you are," she says. "You're always writing. I've just been explaining how when we leave school you're going to do it professionally."

"Hopefully," I add. And then, to show I'm not the only one in my family with big ambitions, I say: "Meg's going to be fashion designer."

"No, I'm not." Meg rolls her eyes and turns back to Abdul.

"I hate writing," Lateef says cheerfully. "I get bored. Uncle Jim's always saying I need to make more effort with school."

"Uncle Jim?" I ask.

"Yeah, he fostered me at first, then officially adopted me a bit later. I've always called him Uncle." He glances around the room, his expression suddenly serious. "I was like these guys when I got here. No family, just arrived in the country. It kind of messes with your head. I got moved around a lot for the first few months, before Uncle Jim took me in."

"How long ago did you come here . . . to England?" I ask.

"Seven years," Lateef says. He smiles. "So, Jo March . . . I've never met a real-life writer before."

I smile back. "I've never met a refugee. Though my mum has. She used to be a social worker." I nod in the vague direction I last saw Mum. "She's over there somewhere."

"What about your dad?" Lateef asks.

"He's in Syria. Is that where you're from?"

"Iraq," Lateef says.

"My dad isn't . . . he just looks after people; he's a humanist minister," I say quickly. I'm not exactly on top of Middle Eastern politics, but Mum and Dad have strong views about westerners going into countries and trying to boss everyone who lives there – and I don't want Lateef to think Dad is like that.

"You must miss him," Lateef says. His dark eyes meet mine and, in that moment, it feels like he can see right into the saddest corner of my heart.

The chattering and clinking sounds of the room whirl around us.

"Do you live in Ringstone?" I ask at last.

"Yeah, on Fishtail Lane," Lateef says, eyes twinkling.

My jaw drops. "No way!" I shriek. "*We* live on Fishtail Lane too." Out of the corner of my eye I catch sight of Meg's head turning. She's frowning, presumably at my loudness.

"Lateef lives on the same street as us," I hiss at her.

"OK, but you don't have to tell *everyone* in the room," Meg snaps. "You . . . you always take up so much *space* when you talk, Jo."

"Then it's lucky," Lateef says quickly, catching my eye, "that Jo obviously has so many interesting things to say."

He winks at me. I grin. Meg rolls her eyes.

"I already knew you lived on Fishtail Lane actually," Lateef goes on. "I saw you moving in a couple of weeks ago. You'll find that when it comes to the big social events in Ringstone, nothing much get pasts me."

We both laugh.

Meg now leans across the table. "So, why haven't you come over to visit us before, Lateef?" she asks.

"Too shy," Lateef says. "Too many pretty girls to deal with."

Meg giggles.

"Lateef?" A burly man in a dark suit, with pink, jowly cheeks and tousled grey hair is calling from the end of the table. He is frowning and looking at his watch, his voice deep and gruff. "Time to go."

Lateef jumps up. "'Course, Uncle." He glances down at me and Meg, lowering his voice. "We're going to visit some of his family. Dull as. Back in a few days, maybe see you then?" He bounces off.

"He seems nice," Meg says approvingly.

I nod, my head spinning.

Because I have a sense, though I can't explain why, that I've just met the person who's going to be my best friend in the whole world.

Chapter 3

Almost a week goes past and we don't see Lateef, though I do wander up and down Fishtail Lane a couple of times, wondering which house is his. Presumably he's still away from home, with Uncle Jim's family. Whatever, I'm certain he'll be in touch soon. I don't tell my sisters how I felt when I met him – they'd just tease me and make out that I *liked* him. Which is *so* not what this is about. Seriously, handsome and charming as he is, I don't fancy Lateef. I don't think about him that way. I just. . . It's hard to describe, but it feels like Lateef understands me in a way that nobody else ever has.

Does that sound crazy? After just one meeting?

Maybe it is; maybe I'm exaggerating the connection

between us. The truth is that I've always found it easier to make friends with boys instead of girls. At our last school, Meg and Amy had these cliques of girls they hung around with, and even Beth had two or three special girlfriends. But I always played mostly with the boys – football in the playground when we were at primary school and more recently just hanging out together and enjoying the banter. I like the way boys can be rude about each other without getting all offended. Most girls don't seem to get that it's just teasing, done for fun. Nothing to fall out over.

Girls fall out all the time over everything. At least that's how it seems to me.

Which means that my first reaction is to say no thanks, when Mrs Gardiner – who organized the Refuge Now charity lunch – calls Mum on Boxing Day and asks if Meg and I would like to come to her daughter Sallie's New Year's Eve party. Meg is delighted, but I'm not. I can just imagine what it will be like – an overheated living room full of gossipy knots of girls who won't know what to make of me. In the end I agree to go, to keep Mum happy – she thinks it'll be a great way to make friends.

For the next few days the party takes over as our main topic of conversation in the house. Amy is furious she can't come – as she reminds us on an hourly basis.

"It's *so* unfair," she says repeatedly.

"But everyone at the party will be older," Meg tells her with more patience than I can manage. "They'll be *our* age, in our years at school."

At the mention of our new school both Beth and Amy fall silent. I get how they're feeling, not that I'd let on. We're all nervous about starting a new school. It's hard to walk in somewhere different, especially when it's not even at the beginning of the school year. I know Beth's been particularly anxious about it. I try not to think about it – after all, what's the point in imagining problems before they happen. I'd rather imagine all the fun stuff that I can do.

Not that Sallie Gardiner's New Year's Eve party qualifies as fun in my book. My greatest fear is that we'll turn up and I'll be faced with a bunch of overdressed girls and no boys to talk to at all. Meg spends two solid days obsessing over what she's going to wear. I couldn't care less.

New Year's Eve arrives and Beth and I are helping Meg to get ready – she still hasn't decided what to wear. Amy is off somewhere else in the house, sulking probably.

"Trouble is, I don't know how smart to go," Meg moans, pulling more clothes out of the wardrobe she and I share. She holds up three tops, one after the other, throwing each in turn on the floor. "The Gardiners have loads of money. Mrs Gardiner's outfit at the Christmas lunch must have cost hundreds."

"Mum always says you should wear what you feel comfortable in," Beth suggests timidly from my bed, where she is curled up next to me like a kitten.

"Well, she never had to meet a load of unknown girls from her future school at a party in a strange new town with only rubbish, out-of-date clothes to wear." Meg chucks yet another rejected top on the floor.

"I'm not sure I'd describe Ringstone as *strange*," I muse, letting my gaze drift to the pictures above my bed: an array of postcards and photos of the places I want, one day, to visit, from the Taj Mahal to the Grand Canyon to Notre Dame in Paris. "Ringstone seems more dull than str—"

"I just mean I don't know how the girls *act* here," Meg snaps.

"Girls are the same everywhere," I say. " I don't get why you're so bothered. I'm going in black trousers and this top, and who cares what anyone thinks?"

Meg casts an appraising eye over my blue cold-shoulder top. It was once hers of course; I never buy new clothes for myself. She narrows her eyes.

"Is that *food*?" she demands, pointing to a tiny yellowish mark on the shoulder.

"No." I grimace. "It's pollen, from lilies at Aunt Em's."

Meg rolls her eyes. "For goodness' sake, Jo," she sighs.

"It's fine," I insist. "I'll keep it covered with my scarf."

Meg shakes her head. "Your big wool scarf will look stupid with that top."

"How are you going to do your hair, Meg?" Beth asks quickly.

I shoot her a grateful glance, knowing she's trying to deflect Meg's attention away from the shortcomings of my outfit.

"I was thinking 'up-do' earlier, but now I'm all about curls," Meg says, pausing for a second to smooth her fair hair off her face. She shoots me an envious look. "I wish I had thick hair that stays in one style like yours, Jo. My hair's a nightmare." She sighs. "OK." She yanks a pale green shirt out of the wardrobe and holds it up next to pair of turquoise trousers. "There," she says. "If I cut the bottoms off the trousers I'll get a frayed hem *and* they'll be the right length."

I stare at the clothes. I would never have thought of altering the trousers, or pairing them with that top, but the colours actually complement each other perfectly. Meg really does have an eye for this sort of thing. She totally should be a fashion designer.

"Nice," I say.

"All I need now are some heels. . ." Meg says, laying the outfit on her bed. "*High* heels."

"Mum won't like you wearing those," Beth says, sitting up with an anxious frown.

She's right. Mum hates high heels and has forbidden us to wear them. She says they make girls vulnerable and are a way of limiting your potential "whether you need to run away from danger or climb a mountain".

"*What* heels?" I ask. I don't possess anything that could be remotely identified as a high-heeled shoe and, as far as I know, Meg doesn't either, despite having fought with Mum over the issue many times.

"These." Meg bends down and draws a cardboard shoebox from the back of the wardrobe. I hadn't noticed it before, but then I generally spend about two seconds getting dressed – usually just selecting jeans or trousers from my quarter section of the hanging space, then yanking a T-shirt or a jumper (depending on the weather) out of my one drawer.

Meg opens the box and reveals a pair of spindly silver open-toed sandals. They sparkle in the light – undeniably pretty but also, to my eyes at least, hopelessly impractical.

"Where did you get those?" I demand.

"Charity shop," Meg explains. "They were only a few quid."

"Mum won't let you wear them," Beth says, her frown deepening.

Meg tosses her head. "She won't know, will she?" She fixes Beth with a glare. Beth nods quickly.

Meg slides the shoes into her bag and tugs on a pair of canvas flats.

"Jo, will you do my hair?"

"If I must," I groan.

Meg plugs in her tongs. They're an ancient set she got off a friend at our old school. The heating element on them doesn't work properly – they get super-hot, super quickly – so Meg doesn't use them much, mostly only for special occasions, like tonight.

Beth slips away to help Mum with supper and

Meg sits in front of the little mirror at the dressing table. I've heated the tongs and I start working my way around Meg's head, winding her hair around the handles.

Meg pores over her phone. I can't see what she's looking at, but she's totally absorbed. I take another strand of hair and apply the tongs, but my thoughts start drifting to Rodriguo and Rachel. Perhaps he should actually attempt to break into her boarding school – maybe by climbing up on to the roof and letting himself down through the chimney.

Suppose he picked a chimney that was being lit for a fire. He could climb halfway down, dirty and choking on the soot, before the smoke started to rise. Then it would be a desperate race against time to make it back up and out of the chimney before the fire took hold.

I can see him now, his dark hair clamped to his forehead with sweat, love for Rachel spurring him on. It's a scene so vivid I can almost smell the fire nipping at his heels, his heart pounding as he—

"Jo! *Jo!*" Meg's cry hauls me back from my dream world. I jump and look down at the tongs. To my horror, a thin curl of smoke rises from the hair still tightly wound round the handles.

"What's that smell?" Meg shrieks, as the unmistakable aroma of burning hair fills the room.

Meg jumps up, pulling away from me. I drop the tongs, my eyes fixed on Meg's soft blonde waves. She clutches her scalp and, to our horror, a few long, blonde strands come away in her fingers. The hair on the rest of her head looks frizzy and wild.

"You've burned my hair, you *idiot!*" she yells.

"It's not that bad," I say. "Hardly even notice—"

"What's happened?" Amy flies into the room, her eyes thrilling to the drama.

Beth and Mum are right behind her. "What on earth?" Mum says.

"Look!" Meg gestures dramatically to the back of her head.

"It's nothing," I insist.

The others crowd around.

Beth claps her hand over her mouth.

"Your hair is *ruined,* Meg," Amy says with theatrical relish. "*Totally* ruined."

Chapter 4

Of course, Meg's hair isn't ruined. It actually looks quite pretty once Mum has curled the rest and put a couple of strategic pins in place. Trust Meg to be able to pull off singed hair. But it doesn't stop her from complaining about how clumsy I am the whole way to the party.

After dreading the whole idea of Sallie Gardiner's party, I'm pleasantly surprised when we turn up at her house and find it full of ordinary-looking girls *and* plenty of boys, all my age or Meg's.

"What a relief," Meg whispers, as Mrs Gardiner leaves us in the hallway in order to seek out Sallie. "I can't see a single designer outfit."

I shrug. I wouldn't know a designer outfit if it bit

me. Still, Meg's right. The kids here seem a lot like the ones back at our old school. And, though none of the Gardiner's furniture is as threadbare or shabby as ours, the sofa and chairs I can see through the open door opposite look comfortable and lived-in, not anything like the stark, minimalist styles I was expecting.

Meg rests her hand on my shoulder for balance while she quickly switches her shoes. As she slips on the high heels hidden in her bag, Sallie Gardiner appears, with a smile on her face and two cute little boys about two years old, in matching dungarees.

"Hello," Meg says, her face lighting up – she loves kids. She bends down to talk to the toddlers. "What are your names?"

The boys smile, blinking up at her.

"Meg, meet Tom and Ted," Sallie explains. "My twin brothers. They've got to go to bed, but Mum's letting me show them to everyone first. Aren't they cute?"

I roll my eyes. Sallie makes them sound like a couple of fashion accessories.

"Oh, they are so adorable." Meg chatters away to the little boys, making silly faces at each one in turn – which makes them laugh – then glancing up at Sallie. "I love your dress and those *earrings*."

I sneak away and drift outside into the big garden, lit on both sides with fairy lights, and that's when I see Lateef. He's standing and chatting with a tall, blond boy whose curls glint in the lights from the house. It's chilly out here and my breath mists in front of my face. Lateef looks over and sees me. He grins like we've known each other for ever, and I smile back, filling with delight that he's here. Lateef grabs the other boy by the arm and leads him over.

"Hey," I say.

"Jo March, we were just talking about you," Lateef says.

The tall blond boy laughs. "Lateef's hardly stopped," he says, and Lateef pokes him in the chest.

"I was saying how cool it is to have a bunch of girls in our road," Lateef goes on. "It's so boring at home, especially when Uncle Jim makes me stay in just because of a stupid cold." I notice that the tip of his nose is a bit pink. "That's why I haven't been round. By the way, this is Tiny." Lateef indicates the boy beside him. I wonder, vaguely, why he's called Tiny when he's so tall. Then I realize that, of course, is the joke and I'm glad I didn't ask my question out loud.

"How many sisters do you have?" Tiny asks,

ruffling his untidy hair. His voice is surprisingly deep.

"Three," I say. "Meg's the only one here tonight – she's inside." I indicate back to the house. "The others are at home."

"Wow," Tiny says. "That's a lot of you. Er, wow."

Lateef pokes him in the chest again. "Jo March doesn't have a drink," he points out.

"I'll get you one," Tiny offers quickly, and disappears into the crowd before I can thank him.

"Tiny's really excited you're here." Lateef looks straight at me, his dark brown eyes sparkling. We're almost the same height; Lateef barely a centimetre or two taller. "I am too. I was hoping you'd be at this party, Jo March."

Embarrassed, I shrug. "Why do you keep calling me Jo March, like . . . my whole name?"

Now it's Lateef's turn to shrug. "Dunno really, maybe 'cos I think it's the coolest name I've ever heard. For the coolest person." He laughs. There's no awkwardness in his manner. No hint of shyness. I think he might be the most straightforward person I've ever met. And maybe the most charming.

"I'm not that cool," I say.

"I would disagree," Lateef says. "But the name's got

to help. And you're a writer, which makes you even cooler. What d'you want to write?"

So, he's remembered. I hesitate. Normally when people ask me that question I fumble around, keeping it vague, only half-answering. Normally I don't want to expose my dreams, to risk the questioner trampling on them. But today I reply with the truth.

"I want to write a really great novel," I say. "One that means something, that matters, that people remember."

"OK," Lateef says, his eyes locked on mine, his voice totally matter-of-fact and sincere. "And I'm sure you will, Jo March."

"Why?"

"Because you look like you can do anything." He glances back at the house, just as Tiny reappears clutching three cans of lemonade. "And because you've obviously got a great family behind you. Your mum was so cool, at the refugee lunch. Everyone I spoke to said what a great listener she was. And I've seen you walking along our street with your sisters – you're always laughing like you're having a great time."

I stare at him. I had no idea he was paying us so much attention. "We get on each other's nerves a lot too," I point out. "So what happened to *your* family back in Iraq?" As soon as the words are out I flush. I might feel like I've known Lateef for ever, but I know enough from things Mum and Dad have told me to know that the answer to my question may be unthinkably horrific.

A brief look of pain crosses Lateef's expressive face and I inwardly curse my runaway tongue. "My family didn't make it from home," he says quietly. "My parents sent me and my brothers on ahead on a boat, but I'm the only one who got here."

"Oh my . . . that's . . . that's awful." I wince as I speak. "I'm so sorry—"

"It's fine," Lateef says quickly. "You don't have to know what to say. Yes, it was . . . is awful. But I'm lucky. Like I told you, Uncle Jim fostered me, then adopted me so I'm—"

"Here you are." Tiny comes over and hands me a lemonade. He spills a little as he drinks from his own can, wiping his mouth afterwards self-consciously, then launches into a rant about the music playing inside and how mainstream and awful it is, and how Sallie should have asked him to DJ instead. I'm not really listening. I'm thinking about Lateef losing his entire family and having to have to start again in a strange new country with a different language and a whole other culture.

Until this moment I'd thought that my life was full of incident and adventure, from the squabbles with my sisters to the upheaval of moving last month and the daily fears for Dad, on the other side of the world in a war zone. But now I realize that compared to Lateef, nothing very significant has happened to me at all.

An hour or two pass. Lateef and I talk about everything from the music we like – both of us are into indie dance stuff – and the school I'm about to start at, which Lateef already goes to and claims rather vaguely is "OK, if you like that sort of thing". We talk about Meg, Beth and Amy too. A lot. Lateef – who has never had any sisters himself – seems fascinated by the idea of my all-girl family.

It gets too cold to stand outside any longer so we go back inside, where Lateef introduces me to a bunch of teenagers from the town, most of whom go to the same school as Lateef and – soon – me. I spot Meg with Sallie Gardiner and some other girls, laughing and talking. Her cheeks are pink as she waves at me. I lose sight of her for about an hour or so until she appears at my elbow, her forehead creased and her eyes dark with pain.

"Jo" she hisses, tugging my arm and pulling me to one side. "Look!"

I peer down. The heel of one silver sandal has snapped half off and is hanging by what looks like a thin thread of cloth and glue.

"They're ruined," I say.

"I know." Meg grimaces. "But it's my ankle. It really hurts."

I open my mouth to point out that if she will wear such stupid shoes she's bound to end up twisting her ankle, then stop myself. Meg's face is white as milk. She must really be in pain.

"Can you make it home?" I ask.

Meg bites her lip. "I'm not sure," she whispers.

"I'll help," Lateef offers, putting down his drink. He's been watching us with interest. "It's only a few streets and if you put your arms around me and Jo, you can keep the weight off your foot."

Meg looks at him, uncertain. "What about the party?"

Lateef shrugs. "It'll finish soon anyway. Sallie told me. Her parents were really strict about it ending at eleven."

"OK. Thank you," Meg says, her face flushing with relief.

"It's fine." Lateef waves away her thanks. "I promised Uncle Jim I'd be home early 'cos of my cold."

"Plus. . ." I wink at him. "Plus, Lateef can't get enough of us, can you, Lateef?"

"Busted." Lateef grins at me. "You ready, Jo March?"

We get home in about fifteen minutes. I've wondered a few times since meeting Lateef exactly where on Fishtail Lane he lives. It's a fairly long road and – though our own little cottage is almost on the pavement with its tiny, paved front yard – most of the houses here are twice as big and set back from the road behind gravel drives and banks of trees.

"Want to know which one's mine?" Lateef asks, as though reading my mind.

I nod. Lateef points across the road and my jaw drops. The house he's indicating is almost opposite our own, but it's so secluded behind a row of tall trees and a gravel drive and so massive that I had previously only noticed the row of top windows and assumed they belonged to some kind of institutional building.

Mum appears as Meg limps through our hallway,

her eyes immediately alight with concern. I'm suddenly aware of how small and narrow the hall is, especially with all our coats and scarves bulging out from their pegs on the wall, but Lateef doesn't seem to notice.

"Hello, Mrs March," he says with a smile. "I'm Lateef, we met at the refugee Christmas lunch. Poor Meg tripped and twisted her ankle, so I helped Jo walk her home."

"Thank you, Lateef." Mum smiles back. She turns to Meg, who winces as she places her injured foot on the bottom step. "Oh, goodness, Meg, you poor love. Why don't you rest on the sofa for a bit before attempting the stairs?"

As Mum helps Meg into the living room, Lateef hovers in the hallway. "I'll say goodnight, then. Will you come over and visit soon?" He points through the open doorway, across to his house. "My room's the last one at the top there."

"Sure," I say. "Thanks." I watch him cross the road, then I shut the door and wander up the stairs.

The bedroom I share with Meg is at the front of our cottage. The window is small but I open it and lean out, looking across to the top of Lateef's house. The room at the end is lit up. Lateef's room. I reach for my phone and flash the torch on and off a couple of times.

I've got no reason to think he'll either understand or respond. But, somehow I'm sure he will. I watch and wait. And then, just a few seconds later, the light in the room goes off and then on again a few times in quick succession. *He got it*, I think to myself, beaming. And then I realize how natural that feels – like, *of course* Lateef got it.

He was bound to get it because, even though we've hardly spent any time together, he somehow understands me like he's known me all my life.

Chapter 5

I'm hunched over my laptop, fingers flying as I write. I only stop, brimming with impatience, to pummel the stupid, sticky *r* key. In real life I'm on my bed but in my imagination I'm with Rodriguo. My heart races as I picture him tip-toeing through Rachel's boarding school, trying to find her dormitory. Meanwhile, Rachel herself is trying to escape out of the window. One of the teachers spots her but as he goes to stop her, he sees Rodriguo and goes after him instead. Rodriguo hears the floor *creak* and he spins around, dropping his torch. The corridor is plunged into darkness and a harsh voice in the shadows calls out: "Stop! Who's there! I have a gun!"

"Jo! *Jo!*"

I look up. Mum is standing over me, shaking her head fondly.

"Didn't you hear me calling you?" she asks. There is affection as well as exasperation in her voice.

I stare at her, still immersed in Rodriguo's plight. I've half a mind to let him be shot – just a graze – something that means Rachel will have to put her own escape plan on hold. Though any kind of wound will make it harder for them to get away, of course. To be honest I'm putting off their escape from the school because I don't know what will come after it.

Mum sits down at the end of the bed. The window beyond is frosted with white sparkles, a line of condensation creating what look like bubbles along the bottom of the glass.

"Aunt Em rang," Mum says. "She wants you to pick up her order of silk cushions from Aspen's on the High Street."

"She wants me to go there *now*?" I groan.

"Yes, she's got friends coming round to play bridge and she needs the cushions, apparently. You've got just under an hour to get to the shop, then drop the cushions at her house, so—"

"But I'm *writing*," I mutter resentfully. "Can't one of the others go?"

Mum folds her arms and gives me one of her sterner looks. "Jo. You said you'd run errands for Aunt Em when we moved here."

"But—"

"Meg helps with the cooking and the laundry, Beth cleans the bathroom and Amy loads the dishwasher and takes out the rubbish." Mum's tone is gentle but steely. "You're the one who *suggested* helping out Aunt Em. You said you wanted something to get you out of the house."

"It's not fair," I protest. "Aunt Em's a dictator."

"No, she's not," says Mum. "She's super busy at work which makes her stressed, then she comes home and she's lonely and isolated in that big house of hers. Plus. . ."

She lets her sentence trail off but I know what she was going to say. *Plus, she lent us the deposit to rent this house. We owe her.*

I sit back. Dad's older sister, Emmeline March, only ever known as Aunt Em by all of us, used to terrify me when I was little. She still does scare Beth. All pursed lips and disapproving attitude. I don't find her scary any more - just difficult and cranky. She's totally dedicated to her career as the marketing director of a big finance company and she's always buying expensive stuff for herself and her house – though she often makes out money is tight.

"Aspen's is on the left bit of the High Street. Just a couple of minutes past the library and almost opposite Tesco's," Mum goes on. "If you leave now you'll be back within the hour." She pats my knee. "Go on."

In spite of my objections, it's actually nice to be outside, the cold air crisp and fresh in my lungs. I hurry towards the High Street, tugging my tartan cap over my ears. It's not technically my cap; Meg and I found it in the back of our wardrobe when we moved. Meg shrieked and pronounced it "beyond hideous" but I think it's kind of jaunty.

The centre of Ringstone is completely different from the neighbourhood in London where we used to live. For a start, there's a proper town centre with a clock tower at the main junction and a High Street running through it. To the east, where we live, a lot of the shops are boarded up. I pass a pound store and a grocery shop, the sun glinting off their dirty windows. Beyond the clock tower, towards West Ringstone, the shops are smarter and more brightly coloured with fresh paint on the doors and window frames. This is where I'm going to find Aspen's. I pass little boutiques stuffed with old-lady dresses, a kitchen shop with a row of those brightly coloured mixers they use on *Bake Off* in the window and two jewellers next door to each other.

I'm not interested in any of these and pass by without breaking my stride. But then I come to Bookbound bookshop, and what I see displayed in the entrance not only makes me stop but actually takes my breath away.

Right at the front is a display of Rowena Riddell's *Blacktower* series with the latest book in the series at the centre, underneath a picture of the author herself. I've seen photos of Rowena Riddell before. She's maybe thirty to thirty-five with long black hair. In this particular picture her hair is all to the side, held in place with a red clip that matches her scarlet jumper. A small, mysterious smile creeps across her lips as she looks into the camera with sparkling eyes.

But it's not the books or the photo that draws my attention the most. It's the sign underneath them that reads:

Rowena Riddell will be signing the latest book in her Blacktower *series next Tuesday.*

Next Tuesday is just six days away, the night before term begins.

I scan the notice anxiously for the time; thank goodness. The signing is at four p.m., so I won't be forced into an argument with Mum over going out late the night before I begin at a new school.

I almost skip the rest of the way to Aspen's, barely noticing the fact that the air is now bitingly cold. I'm in such a dream world that I've no sooner signed for Aunt Em's four silk cushions than I almost leave them on the counter, causing the poor guy serving to have to shout out to me.

I only drop one cushion once on my way to Aunt Em's, which isn't bad considering I'm trying to balance all four of them in my arms as Aspen's didn't have bags big enough. I turn the damp edge of the dropped cushion away as I pass them to Aunt Em's housekeeper and scurry off home before Aunt Em can stop me.

Snowflakes are fluttering down as I pass the clock tower and within minutes the flutter has turned to a deluge. I'm soaked through, though my tartan cap at least keeps my head warm. By the time I turn on to our road there's a thin layer of white over everything, from the wheelie bins set out for rubbish collection to the rooftops far above my head.

Lateef is outside his house, wheeling a bin into position at the end of the gravel drive. I can see, looking across the road, that Amy has already put out ours. I scoop a handful of fresh snow off the hedge I'm passing, mould it into a small, hard ball, and chuck it at Lateef.

I've always been good at throwing and catching but even I'm surprised at how accurate my aim is. The tiny snowball catches Lateef squarely on the side of the neck – the only bit of his body that's exposed above his black jacket and below his grey beanie.

"Hey!" Lateef slaps his hand over his neck, spinning round.

I double over laughing. A second later, he's cracking up too, scooping a handful of snow and running at me, trying to shove it down my neck. I reach around to make another snowball but there isn't really enough snow. Anyway, Lateef is pinning my arms down. He's panting for breath with the effort and we're both still laughing. Lateef turns me to face him. He's barely taller than I am, but surprisingly strong. We're so close I can see the snowflakes on his eyelashes.

Lateef stares at me for a second, then lets me go. I spring back, grinning.

"Good to see you, Jo March. Where've you been?"

"To the shops for my aunt." The mention of "shops" reminds me of the sign in the bookshop window and I tell him all about Rowena Riddell's book signing next week.

Lateef says he's never heard of her. "I told you already," he says, laughing at my outraged expression. "I'm not a big reader. Movies though, *now* you're talking."

"Well, I love movies too," I say. "I just love stories, really."

"You know we have a home cinema in the basement? It's really cool."

"Seriously?" I'm wide-eyed. I've heard of people having cinemas in their houses, but I've never actually been in one.

"Seriously." Lateef grins, a dimple appearing in his cheek. "Come round now. Check it out."

I hesitate – I know the others will kill me if I don't ask them along too. But it's too good an offer to turn down. And living in a small house without much money and so many siblings means sharing almost everything. I want to keep Lateef and his fancy house for myself – just for now.

"OK, thanks," I say. We make our way up Lateef's

driveway. As the whole house comes into view my jaw drops.

It's even more enormous than I'd realized: three massive storeys with at least six windows across each level, surrounded by lawn and a thick copse of trees on both sides.

"Jumping Jack Jellybeans," I mutter under my breath, borrowing a classic phrase from the *Blacktower* series. Lateef and his adopted family must be *really* rich.

And, for the first time since I met Lateef, I feel nervous.

Chapter 6

My nerves don't lessen as I follow Lateef through the wood-panelled entrance hall and down a flight of stone steps to the home cinema. It's enormous. It runs under at least half the house, with a massive screen at one end that's bigger than some I've seen in actual cinemas! The walls are carpeted with the same thick, soft purple fabric as the floor, and the seats are stepped in four rows, each of which is six seats wide. I do the maths quickly in my head.

"You could have twenty-four people in here," I gasp, unable to keep the awe out of my voice.

"That doesn't happen very often," Lateef says, clearly enjoying my wonderment. "A couple of my birthday parties maybe and once a year when Uncle

Jim hosts one of his charity functions. He's a lawyer but he does lots of stuff for kids' charities in his spare time."

"Wow," I say.

"Check this out." Lateef presses a button and the far wall slides back to reveal a long set of shelves, stacked with DVDs. "Most of our newer films are downloads, but Uncle Jim has a collection going back eighty years."

I examine the shelves. The films are arranged in date order, a set of black-and-white movies I've never heard of at the start.

"Wow," I say again.

Lateef chuckles. "D'you want to get a drink? Rosalie – she looks after the house – makes this great lemonade, like, proper stuff. Tastes awesome. And homemade cookies."

"Sure." I follow Lateef back up to the ground floor and into a large kitchen with gleaming stainless-steel surfaces. It's at least three times as big as our kitchen and way tidier. "Is it just you living here and your d—" I hesitate.

"Uncle Jim?" Lateef finishes for me. "We talked about me calling him 'Dad' but I remember my actual father really clearly, so it didn't feel right calling someone else that. . . Anyway, yup, just the two of us. Uncle Jim was married and they had a daughter, but his wife and the daughter died in a car accident a long time ago." He pauses. "I never knew either of them. It had a big impact on Jim. People think he's a bit rough, rude even . . . but he's just shy and . . . and he doesn't say, but I know he still misses them a lot."

I don't know what to say; it's so incredibly sad. I imagine losing Dad and shiver. I wander across the kitchen to a set of folding doors that are just slightly ajar. I push the doors open to reveal a dining area with a massive wooden table running down the centre.

"Uncle Jim likes the doors closed. He's fussy about stuff like that," Lateef explains. "Says that there's no point wasting money heating rooms we don't use, that smaller spaces make the place more cosy."

Cosy is probably the last word I'd have chosen to describe either the neat, sparkling kitchen or this smart dining room with its big glass cabinets full of ornaments and photos. There's a full-sized upright piano beyond the table to the left-hand end of the dining room. I stare at the glossy white wood; I can almost see my face in the shine of it. A vase of flowers stands on the piano lid, which is perfectly smooth apart from a small chip in one corner. A trio of portraits hang on the wall above: a middle-aged man and woman, formally dressed, on either side and a girl in the centre.

"Is that them?" I ask, staring at the picture of the man. In the painting he's wearing a three-piece navy suit, and his hair is dark and slicked back from his narrow face. He looks handsome and doesn't bear much relation to the grey-haired, ruddy-cheeked person with the stern eyes who called Lateef away at the charity lunch.

"That's them." Lateef follows my gaze. "The girl's name was Francesca."

I move closer, studying the portrait of the child. She has the same shiny dark hair as her father and soft grey eyes.

"How old was she when she died?" I ask.

"Fifteen," Lateef explains. "Our age."

I shiver again, thinking how terrible it would be to lose someone that way: the shock of it, the sudden empty space in the world where they used to be. I look back at the picture of Lateef's Uncle Jim. He isn't smiling in his portrait. In fact, he's frowning. It strikes me that he sounded cross at the charity lunch too.

"He looks really fierce," I said. "And *very* strict. I bet he can be a nightmare when—"

"A nightmare, am I?" a loud male voice booms behind me.

I spin round, a flush leaping up my neck and burning my cheeks.

Uncle Jim is standing in the doorway. He's obviously just walked in as he's wearing an overcoat with a dusting of snow along the shoulders. His grey hair is plastered over his damp face and his eyes glitter dangerously.

He still isn't smiling.

Chapter 7

"I didn't. . . I'm. . . I. . ." I stammer. "I was just. . ."

"Hey, Uncle," Lateef says cheerfully. "This is Jo March, from over the road. She was at the refugee charity lunch and—"

"I remember," Uncle Jim barks. He's wearing a suit under his overcoat, similar to the one in the portrait. He was formally dressed at the lunch too. "So you don't like my picture, young lady, is that it?"

"No! It's just. . ."

"Just the subject?" Uncle Jim says curtly. "Go on, then, tell me what you make of us." He points at the three pictures. "Me and my wife and our daughter. What do the paintings tell you about us?"

My heart beats fast as I turn back to the pictures

on the wall. I catch Lateef's eye and he gives me a reassuring wink. I take a deep breath, trying not to let Uncle Jim intimidate me.

"Well," I say, "you come across as fierce and stern in your picture, but your wife looks kind." I glance at him, but his face gives nothing away. "And your daughter – Francesca, isn't it? – looks like she was quite dreamy and shy. She reminds me of my younger sister a bit – shy around most people, but if she trusts you she'll chatter away." I pause. "Lateef told me they passed away. I'm very sorry."

There's a long silence and when Uncle Jim speaks again there's a catch in his voice.

"You're right about my wife. She *was* kind. And you're right about Franny too," he says, "she was shy and liked nothing better than to play that." He nods at the beautiful piano. "She was good too, worked hard at it." He casts a glance at Lateef and gives a wry smile. "Not like some people."

"Do you play, Lateef?" I ask him, glad to turn the subject.

"Kind of," Lateef says with a rueful grin. "I don't practise as much as I should."

"You don't practise at all." Uncle Jim snorts.

"Anyway, I'm sorry I startled you, Jo. I'm James Laurence, but please call me Uncle Jim." He strides forward and holds out his hand for me to shake, which I do, making sure my hand grips his properly. Dad's always saying that there's very little that makes a worse first impression than a limp handshake.

"We appreciated you girls coming to the charity lunch," Uncle Jim carries on. "A long time ago, my late wife used to run the local branch of Refuge Now. She did the job that Liz Gardiner does now. It's important to me to support their good work." He pauses. "I spoke to your mother at the lunch. Seems like a fine lady. Must be hard for her with your father abroad." He smiles at last, and his face softens. "I bet you girls are a handful, too. Three of you, are there?"

"Four," I explain.

He raises his eyebrows. "Goodness, four girls?"

"Yes, Meg's the oldest, she's into design and style, very talented and beautiful and kind. Amy's the youngest. She likes drawing and having nice stuff and impressing people; though, to be fair, she's incredibly loyal too. And then there's Beth. . ." I trail off, unsure how to describe her.

"And what's Beth like?" Uncle Jim raises a bushy eyebrow.

"She's the opposite of me. Always careful." I say slowly. "About what she does and what she says, whereas I rush into things. And she's shy, like your daughter was. That's who Francesca's picture made me think of, in fact. And Beth loves playing the piano, too. At home we've only got this cronky old keyboard that's like a million years old, but Beth still practises every day."

"Hear that, Lateef? Practising every day. *That's* what it takes."

Lateef shrugs with good humour. "I know, I know – it's just that I'm busy. . ."

I laugh. "Mum would say *that's* an excuse," I say.

To my surprise, stern-looking Uncle Jim lets out a deep chuckle. "You tell him, Jo! His teacher says he's got talent, but he doesn't work at it. And if there's one thing I've learned in thirty-five years as a lawyer it's that you have to work to get anywhere in life." He peers at me. "What's your ambition, Jo?"

"I'm going to be a famous novelist," I say, without hesitation.

Uncle Jim laughs again. "Good for you. Well, you're very welcome here. And so are your sisters.

And if Beth wants to come and play this proper piano here instead of her . . . *cronky* old keyboard, we'd be delighted to have her."

I'm buzzing when I get home, though Aunt Em does her best to bring me down by calling and complaining that I damaged one of her stupid silk cushions earlier.

"What on earth happened, Jo?" Mum asks despairingly.

"I just dropped one on the floor," I explain, demonstrating how it happened using four of the battered cushions from our faded sofa.

"It was only a tiny bit damp in one corner," I insist.

Mum sighs and lets the matter drop.

I help Meg make dinner and, later that evening, I tell Beth about Uncle Jim, our conversation and the portraits above the piano. She listens, wide-eyed.

"It's an awesome piano," I explain. "And Uncle Jim says you can go round there and play it whenever you like."

"I couldn't." Beth's cheeks whiten. She sets down her knitting. "No *way* could I play with people listening."

"Oh, Beth," I say, "you play in front of us all the time."

"That's different. I don't know Lateef or his uncle Jim. I couldn't play in front of *strangers*."

"Well, once you've met them both properly they won't *be* strangers any more, I point out, but" Beth shakes her head.

"So, what's Lateef like now you know him a bit better?" Meg asks, having drifted in towards the end of our conversation.

"He's great, you guys will love him. He lives in this mansion with an actual, proper home cinema and loads of space and expensive stuff, but he's not at all stuck up. And he's been through such a hard time – he lost his entire family when he came here."

"Ooh, what expensive stuff?" Amy asks, following Meg into the room.

"For Pete's sake, Amy," I groan. "Unlike you, I don't spend my time in other people's houses checking out their belongings."

"It must have been a big shock for Lateef, coming from a country where there's conflict and lots of poverty," Beth muses. "And no matter what possessions they have or how big their house is, Lateef's still lost more in his life than he's gained."

"Of course," Amy says with a dismissive wave. "But – if he had to leave his homeland, imagine how *amazing* it must have been for Lateef to be suddenly rich and surrounded by nice things."

"Jeez, you are *so* superficial, Amy," I snap, seriously irritated now. "There's more to life than 'nice things'."

"I'm not superficial. And even if I was I'd rather be superficial than super-chilly-us like *you*," Amy snaps.

"The word is super*cil*ious." I roll my eyes.

"Exactly. And I *know* there's more to life than nice things. I'm just thinking that if he's got so much money and we got to know him *really* well . . . then, well, maybe Uncle Jim might be prepared to pay for me to have a nose job. . ."

At this, Meg and I break into laughter. Even Beth smiles. And Amy, chin firmly stuck in the air, stalks out of the room.

Chapter 8

It's the final weekend before we start at our new school on Wednesday and everyone's making the most of our remaining free time before homework kicks in. Meg has been poring over some old copies of *Vogue* magazine from the eighties and nineties that Aunt Em was throwing out – yawn, fashion. Meanwhile Beth's been knitting like mad and doing lots of piano practice – Mum's organized free lessons at the new school and Beth is worrying already about having to play for a new teacher. As for Amy, she's taken to wandering around the house making irritating comments and staring at herself in the mirror. Well, to be fair, she's also spending a lot of time starting new paintings and drawings, though she does tend to get bored quickly and drop them before they're finished.

I'm the opposite with my writing. I spend ages on my stories, often working for hours to get a single paragraph just right. Right now, for instance, I'm stationed in the kitchen, which is often noisy but has the advantage of being close to food, and I've been writing for the past forty-eight hours with hardly any break: Rodriguo has found Rachel's dormitory at the boarding school now. He didn't get shot, but he sprained both ankles trying to leap from a second-floor window to get away from one of the tutors, who heard him making a noise. He's now hiding out in the caretaker's disused coal shed, which is very dirty, but he can rest his ankles there while Rachel brings him food and water. She's risking a lot to help him, but then he risked a lot to find her. When he can walk again, they're going to escape. At least, they're going to try!

As you've probably guessed, burying myself in my imaginary world is how I deal with *my* anxieties about the new school. Plus I've got Rowena Riddell's signing on Tuesday to look forward to. I was planning on taking *all* my books for her to sign but now I'm thinking I'll just get the new one signed and hopefully a selfie with her too.

I've just finished a scene in which Rachel tenderly bandages Rodriguo's damaged ankles then has to fight off the caretaker's fierce guard dog on her way back to her dormitory, when Amy sticks her head around the door.

"You have to go to Aunt Em's in an hour," she says.

"What?" I look up. "*Why?*"

"She's having a drinks party and wants you to hand out the nibbles." Amy smirks. "Mum says it's 'cos she's got some last-minute guests from work and doesn't want to add to the catering costs by asking for more staff."

Mum herself walks in at this point.

"I *can't* go to Aunt Em's party," I cry, jumping up and knocking my half-drunk mug of tea across the kitchen table. Luckily it misses my laptop and simply splashes a bit over the floor. "I'm about to write the most important scene in my story where Rachel and Rodriguo make their first, proper attempt to escape together."

"Oh, Jo," Mum grabs a tea towel and mops at the table. She hands me a dishcloth so I can clear up what's on the floor. Amy, I notice, has already slunk off. "You'll just have to carry on writing when you get back."

There's no point arguing. Grumbling, I let Mum coax me into a dress so that I'll look presentable at Aunt Em's stupid party. It's actually one of Mum's old pinafore dresses, a beautiful shade of green – which is my favourite colour. Meg helps me team it with a pale grey jumper and DMs, then gives a sigh.

"You don't know how lucky you are, Jo," she says. "That dress is too long for me – I'd look swamped in it."

"I'd happily be less tall if it meant I didn't have to wear a dress ever again," I groan, now struggling to pull a brush through my tangled hair.

Aunt Em's house is bustling when I arrive, with a chef in the kitchen sweating over the canapés and three young men in tuxedoes fussing over trays of food and bottles of wine.

"Very nice, Jo," Aunt Em says when she sees me. "That green suits you."

"Thanks," I say. Aunt Em is dressed, as usual, in her signature black, though instead of her usual uniform of black jeans and a cashmere sweater she's wearing a cocktail dress, knee-length, with a choker of massive diamonds to match the ones on the rings on her fingers.

"What do you need me to do?" I ask, trying to sound helpful.

"Just hand around the trays," Aunt Em says. "And you may say you're my niece and talk about how you've just moved here. But don't pester people. If they're deep in conversation, just move away."

As if I want to talk to her stupid friends anyway!

The evening passes slowly. Very slowly. A few people do ask me about myself, mostly the same two questions: how old am I and where do I go to school? Some are only interested in what canapés I'm serving and the rest actually behave as if I'm not even there, as if the tray I'm carrying is being wafted around by magic!

I can't wait to get home, which is probably why I'm hurrying back to the kitchen with my empty tray, just as one of Aunt Em's guests – clearly someone very important from the way she's been fawning over him all night – walks into the living room.

Wham. I hurtle straight into him, the empty tray catching the glass of red wine in his hand and sending its contents soaring into the air. Time seems to slow down as Aunt Em, the Very Important Guest, and I, watch the liquid arc and spread and land all over the man's crisp, white shirt. Drops spray on to his face.

"Aagh!" Aunt Em shrieks.

The Very Important Guest freezes, wide-eyed with shock.

"Oh my gosh, sorry, I'm so sorry," I gabble, snatching up a napkin from the pile on a nearby table as I advance towards him. I dab at the man's chest, but he backs away, his thin lips pressed together in an expression of extreme distaste.

"Jo!" Aunt Em's ice-cold voice stops me in my tracks.

Our eyes meet. She shakes her head. "I think you can go home now," she snaps.

"Yes, OK, sure, er," I turn to the Very Important Guest again, offering him the wine-stained napkin clutched in my hand. "I really am very sorry."

And with that I duck and hurry away, snatching up my coat and racing out of the house as fast as possible.

Mum is open-mouthed when I tell her what happened. She shakes her head sorrowfully as I describe how the guest and I collided, although when I tell her how he backed away from me as I brandished a napkin at him, her lips twitch and I can tell she's trying not to laugh.

Aunt Em calls later, of course, complaining to

Mum about my "wildness", which puts me in a bad mood. Not for myself so much, but because I hate it when anyone gives Mum a hard time.

The following morning, however, I wake to a message from Lateef saying that he's got three tickets for a preview screening this very afternoon of the latest film adaptation of Rowena Riddell's *Blacktower* series. And do Meg and I want to go with him?

Of course we do. I'm beside myself with excitement at the prospect and spend the whole day looking forward to the movie. Meg – who has a crush on the lead actor – is almost as delirious as I am.

The only thing threatening to spoil our plans is Amy.

Ever since she found out about the screening, she's been whining that it's not fair and that she should be allowed to come with us.

"We can't take you," Meg says in what – as far as I'm concerned – is far too conciliatory a tone. "Lateef only has two spare tickets."

"Not that we'd want you to come anyway," I mutter.

Meg glances sideways at me, an exasperated frown creasing her brow. "Jo, don't be mean."

I glare at Meg, irritated. I know most of the time

Meg finds Amy as irritating as I do, so why does she always take Amy's side in arguments?

"You know what she's like in the cinema," I point out.

"You mean asking about the story during the film?" Meg frowns again. "She hasn't done that for years."

"See?" Amy pouts. "This is *so* unfair, Jo. You wouldn't act like this if it was Beth who wanted to come with you."

"That's because Beth doesn't act like an idiot when she goes out," I snap. "Meg can say what she likes, but I'm *glad* you're not coming to the cinema with us."

Amy's face reddens, two dark red spots emerging on her cheeks. Her eyes glitter dangerously. I brace myself, expecting her to yell at me, tell me how much she hates me or burst into tears. But instead she simply clenches her fists.

"I'll get you for this, Jo," she hisses. And then she stalks out.

I laugh, part relieved that she's gone, part amused by her indignation, part wishing I hadn't been so mean. Of all of us, Amy is normally the one most likely to go into histrionics when she doesn't get her way. That icy tone is new, and it makes me uneasy.

Then I shake myself – Amy is just being dramatic. She might be upset now, but it will all have blown over by tomorrow. And, if it hasn't, I'll apologize then.

As soon as we've left the house I forget all about Amy. It's a sunny day: crisp and chilly but with no sign of rain.

"Are you seriously wearing that tartan cap?" Lateef asks me, a huge grin on his face. He's sporting a three-quarter length black jacket that Meg has already informed me is a Hugo Boss worth over two hundred quid, and swinging a long black umbrella from his hand.

"I know, isn't it hideous?" Meg sighs.

"You two just don't understand my style," I banter back. "And I don't see how you can complain about my cap when you're carrying that ridiculous umbrella, like you're forty-seven, when it isn't even going to rain."

Lateef throws his head back and guffaws. "The umbrella is *my* style," he counters. "Sharp, classic *and* useful. None of which can be said about your cap."

"Whatever." I poke him in the ribs.

This is one of the things I love most about Lateef,

how he gets my humour. I don't have any other friends who I could have this kind of conversation with. Lateef doesn't take what I say personally and I don't feel hurt by his teasing either.

It turns into a brilliant afternoon. The film is amazing. Being at the preview screening is the coolest thing. A couple of the actors from the movie are even here – though not the leading man, much to Meg's disappointment.

Afterwards, Meg spots a friend and goes for a hot chocolate. Lateef and I chat about the movie all the way home. He's completely converted to Rowena's amazing world.

"And that bit at the end, when the best friend turns out to be her long lost sister. . ." Lateef makes a gesture with his hands, spreading them wide to show how the impact of the revelation was just too awesome to be described in words.

"I know, that's my favourite part," I say. "I can't wait for you to read the book – the whole series in fact. You should start with the first one."

"Way ahead of you," Lateef says with a grin. "I've already downloaded the movie of it. I thought we could watch it at mine."

I open my mouth to say he should read the book

first, but Lateef looks so pleased with himself that I can't bring myself to ruin his plan.

"That sounds perfect," I say.

As we turn on to Fishtail Lane, I glance across the road to our house. It's dusk and the lights are already on in the living room though the curtains aren't drawn yet. Mum is sitting alone at the table, writing something. Probably another job application. I feel a twinge of concern. She's been out of work for months now. I peer up at the windows above, wondering idly where Beth and Amy are. There's no sign of them; all the rooms are dark. As I watch, a light goes on in our room. It can't be Meg – she's still out with her friend. Perhaps it's Beth putting our ironing back on our beds.

"Come on, slowpoke," Lateef urges. And forgetting my own home for the moment, I turn and follow Lateef along his drive and into his.

Chapter 9

The hallway of Lateef's house is in darkness, but light glimmers from the dining room and the sound of piano music, gentle and lyrical, drifts towards us. Uncle Jim is in the doorway of the room, presumably watching whoever is playing the piano. He turns towards us as we walk in, his finger to his lips.

Lateef shuts the front door silently behind us. As we draw closer to Uncle Jim, tiptoeing so as to make no noise, I realize that my heart is in my mouth. There's something magical about the moment, about the ethereal music and the soft glow of light – in a room where a girl once played, who is now dead. It is as though her ghost is laying her hands on the keys. I reach the door and peer into the room.

No ghost. But the identity of the actual pianist is no less astonishing.

It's Beth.

Her head is bowed over the piano, her fingers running expertly up and down the keys. She's lost in whatever she is playing, a soft smile on her sweet face.

We've been totally silent, but something – maybe the cold air that's swept into the house after us – makes Beth look up.

Her eyes widen as she sees us all and there's a discordant *twang* as her fingers crash on the keys. She jumps up from the piano, shoulders tensed, as all three of us start speaking at once:

"Bethy, that was beautiful," I say.

"I had no idea you could play like that," says Lateef, sounding awed.

Beth turns to Uncle Jim. "You said you were going out," she says, her face flushing.

"I *was* going out, Beth," Uncle Jim says, a crack in his voice. "But I got delayed upstairs with a phone call and when I came down and heard you, it brought back such... It sounded so lovely... I'm sorry. I couldn't help listening, just for a moment."

Beth hesitates. "That's OK," she stammers, her

kind heart clearly winning the day. "I just hate being listened to."

"You shouldn't," Lateef says with a broad grin. "You're amazing."

Beth's blush deepens to a dark crimson and I swell with pride.

"She's great, isn't she?" I agree. "Like the rest of us all think we're so creative, but Beth's the one with the real gift."

"Oh, Jo," she says, shuffling from foot to foot. "I just practise a lot."

"You're welcome here anytime you want," Uncle Jim says. "It would be a pleasure."

"Thank you." Beth is still fidgeting. She rubs her finger over the chip on the edge of the piano lid. "And thank you, Mr Laurence, for letting me use this beautiful piano. But I have to go now . . . er, Mum needs me at home." And with that she scuttles across the room and brushes past us. The sound of her shoes tapping lightly over the wooden hall floor echoes across the room. A second later the front door opens and closes with a soft *thud*. Another blast of cold air swirls around us.

Uncle Jim stands, staring at the piano, lost in his thoughts.

Lateef tugs at my sleeve. "Come on," he whispers, his eyes on his uncle. "Let's go and watch the movie."

We go down to the home cinema and Lateef puts on the first *Blacktower* movie. I'm not really concentrating on the story. I can't stop thinking about the look of pain in Uncle Jim's eyes as he watched Beth play. It doesn't take a genius to work out that he was reminded of his dead daughter. I've never really thought much about what that kind of loss would feel like. I guess I've been lucky so far, that nobody I love has ever died. We did have a dog once who had to be put down and Beth and Mum cried buckets, but though I felt sad about losing Handsome (Amy was the one who – for some reason I'll never understand – was allowed to give him that ridiculous name) it was never the same searing grief that I know the others felt.

It hurts that Dad is away, of course, and sometimes I'm frightened that though he doesn't fight himself, he might get caught up in the warfare that goes on around him, but in my heart I believe he will come back. I have to.

I'd like to write about that kind of loss one day, but it's scary to imagine and for now I'm happy sticking to Rodriguo and Rachel and their adventures.

Although . . . the look on Uncle Jim's face as he remembered his daughter does make me question the ending I've been planning. . .

I'd thought before that Rodriguo and Rachel needed to escape, to run away together, but perhaps they can appeal to Rachel's father and – because he doesn't want to lose his daughter – he relents and lets Rodriguo be part of her life.

"Yes, that's better than running away," I muse.

"What's that?" Lateef asks.

I look around. The credits for the film are just starting to roll.

"Nothing, thanks for the movie," I say leaping up from the home cinema chair. I'm suddenly desperate to get home and write it all down.

"Are you going already?" Lateef asks. "Don't you want to get some lemonade first? I think there's chocolate cake too."

"No, I've got to get back. But thanks so much for the movie, and the tickets earlier." I hesitate. "And please say goodbye to Uncle Jim too. I'm sorry I said he was a nightmare before . . . he's not, not at *all*."

I don't bother to put my coat on as I race across the road, eager to get back home. It's properly dark now and the curtains in our house have been drawn, slivers of light peeking out around the edges. My story about Rachel and Rodriguo is already over twenty-six thousand words long. I can't wait to get up to my room, fetch my laptop and carry on writing.

I fly inside, letting the front door slam behind me.

"Jo? Is that you?" Mum calls from the living room.

I glance in as I pass. They're all in there: Beth is reading, curled up at Mum's side on the sofa, while Meg sits by the window, examining the buttons on a blouse. Amy is lying stretched out on the floor, apparently engrossed in her phone. She doesn't glance up as I burst in. Is she still upset about me and Meg going to the preview screening earlier? I make a mental note to come down and be super-nice to her as soon as I've got my next chapter down.

"Back in a sec," I shout out, panting as I take the stairs two at a time. I hurtle into the room I share with Meg and snatch my laptop off my bed. It's resting half on the pillow, under the picture of Notre Dame that's pinned on the wall. I have a vague sense that isn't exactly where I left it, but I don't think about this as I thunder back downstairs.

"Could you make any more noise?" Meg yells

out, with a despairing laugh. "It's like living with an elephant."

"Did you eat at Lateef's?" Mum calls.

Ignoring them both I run into the kitchen, which is the only room with a table uncluttered enough for me to work on, and plonk my laptop down. I fetch myself a glass of water while it's firing up, then I scan the desktop for the Word file that contains my Rachel and Rodriguo story.

It isn't there.

I look again, methodically moving every file with the cursor, double-checking to make sure. It *must* be here. It doesn't make any sense that it's gone. My throat tightens as I go over the desktop files a third time. The file definitely isn't here.

My heart thuds with anxiety as I open the cloud and scan my back-up files. Everything else is here, but not my story. I check again. Surely my eyes must be playing tricks on me. It can't have just *vanished*.

Panicking now, I click on *Restore*, but nothing appears. I sit back, my head spinning. It's as if someone has logged on to my computer and permanently deleted the story file from both the hard drive and virtual storage.

But who would do that? And why?

A possible answer curls itself around my heart, squeezing all the breath out of me. Gripping the sides of the kitchen table I rise up and walk to the living-room door.

Beth glances up, smiles at me, then goes back to her book.

Meg, on the other side of the room, also smiles. "Lateef really seemed to enjoy the movie, didn't he?"

I can't answer. Can't speak. Can't form words. Because I'm letting my gaze rest on Amy who is, still, intent on her phone. She isn't looking back at me. I can't see her expression, but her body is stiff with tension. She knows I'm watching her and she can't meet my eyes.

And that tells me everything I need to know.

I stride over and stand in front of her. "Amy?"

She ignores me.

"Amy?" I reach down and take the mobile out of her hand.

She springs up, lunging for the phone, but I hold it over my head where she can't reach.

"Give it back!" Amy shrieks.

"What on earth, Jo?" Mum protests. "Don't tease her like that."

"Did you do it?" I say.

"Give it back!" Amy says again, this time more sullenly.

She's not even denying it.

A fury sears through me. I'm white hot with it. I turn to Mum, letting Amy's phone fall on to the carpet where she snatches it up and backs away from me.

"Amy's deleted the story I've been working on since before we moved," I say, tears pricking at my eyes. "Permanently deleted. The back-up and everything."

Across the room Mum blinks, clearly shocked. Beth claps her hand over her mouth. Meg drops the blouse she's holding.

They all stare at my youngest sister.

"Is this true, Amy?" Mum asks.

Amy juts out her chin and shrugs.

"Amy?" Mum's voice is sharp as a knife.

A long pause, then Amy mutters: "Yes. I did it." She looks up defiantly. "You deserved it, Jo; you were so horrible to me earlier. You're *always* picking on m—"

"You evil, evil brat! I'll never forgive you as long as I live!" I lunge for Amy, who ducks under my arm and races out of the room.

I make to go after her, but Mum catches my arm.

"No, Jo," she says.

I'm shaking with rage, but I stop struggling. Even in the heat of my anger I know that I shouldn't be near Amy right now.

"Let me speak to her," Mum says. She hurries out of the room. Meg has already vanished, presumably after Amy.

I sink to the floor, all the fury suddenly ebbing out of me. A small hand clasps mine and I look up into Beth's soft, sad eyes.

"Your brilliant Rachel and Rodriguo story?" she whispers. "It's really all gone? Even the backup?"

I nod, the reality of what I've lost fully sinking in.

"Oh, Jo, I'm so sorry."

And, as Beth squeezes my hand, the hot, bitter tears flood out of me as if they'll never stop.

Chapter 10

"Please, Jo, *please,* I'm so so sorry." Amy's lower lip wobbles tremulously but I don't care.

I refuse to forgive her.

I refuse even to speak to her.

It's been two days since she committed her terrible crime and I'm certain she has no idea how devastated I am. All my work . . . my entire story about Rodriguo and Rachel . . . is gone and there's no way I can get it back. Perhaps if it were just one scene, maybe even a couple of chapters, then I might attempt to rewrite it. But not over twenty-six thousand words. I worked so hard getting them just right and there's no way I'll be able to remember what I put down before, or to write a replacement version that will be as good. That's how I feel now, anyway.

It's like Amy has ripped my heart out.

And nobody understands. They're all sympathetic but they've never tried to write a book. Meg might pore over dress designs but she's never actually made anything, and though Beth and Mum play the piano beautifully, they don't compose music.

They don't understand how my stories are a part of me, at the heart of my being, my *soul*.

"Jo, please talk to me." Amy is crying now. "Please forgive me."

She's standing in the narrow hallway, blocking my way to the front door. I've spent most of the past two days in my room, gazing at the pictures of far-off places above my bed and wishing I could escape to them. I've only been coming out for meals, which Mum insists we all eat together. But this evening I'm going out with Lateef to Rowena Riddell's signing. I've been looking forward to it all week now and there's no way I'm going to let Amy and her spiteful behaviour stop me from enjoying meeting my favourite author of all time.

Who knows? Maybe meeting Rowena Riddell will inspire me to write a new story. I take my black jacket and the tartan cap off the overloaded coat peg by the front door. Amy is still hovering beside me, her hands clasped together, tears streaming down her cheeks.

"Please, Jo," she beseeches.

I glare at her. "Get out of my way," I hiss. Lateef will be here any second and the last thing I want is for him to see Amy weeping and to have to explain why. I'd rather avoid the subject tonight. Concentrate on having fun.

Amy turns and flees, her sobs growing louder as she thunders upstairs. Mum emerges from the kitchen. She's been applying for jobs again. Through the open door I can hear Beth on her little keyboard. Several of the notes stick and the overall sound is horribly tinny, but Beth still fills what she plays with feeling.

"Jo, you need to make up with Amy," Mum says, leaning against the wall with a sigh.

I tug on my jacket. "No," I say, feeling mutinous. "You don't understand. What Amy did was *unforgiveable*."

"It was mean," Mum acknowledges. "But it was done in anger, without real thought of the consequences. Amy isn't a cruel person, she acted in the heat of the moment and—"

"I don't care," I say, my voice rising. "She's destroyed everything I've been working on for the past few months. I won't *ever* be able to recreate it."

"I know," Mum says sympathetically. "And I understand that it feels like the end of the world right now, but it's not worth cutting yourself off from your sister over."

"Isn't it?" The words blurt out of me. I can't believe Mum is taking Amy's side like this.

"No, Jo, listen to me. It was understandable that your first reaction was fury, but you've *been* angry now. You need to let it go."

"Let it *go?*" I gasp. "It's the worst thing that's ever happened to me."

"Then you've led a very fortunate life," Mum says. "Think about Lateef. Imagine losing everything."

I stare at her. She's right, a part of me realizes. Of course I haven't been wrenched away from my entire family. Far from it. But just because he – and lots of other people – are worse off than I am, I don't see why that means I'm not allowed to feel resentful. What Amy did still hurts. Mum has no idea what it feels like to pour your heart into a story and have it be trampled to smithereens.

"That's not fair," I say. "You can't compare my life

with his. What Amy did was wrong. And mean. And totally unprovoked."

"It was definitely wrong and yes, it was mean," Mum agrees. "But you have to bear some responsibility for Amy's anger. She is several years younger than you and eager to join in and instead of welcoming her, or letting her down gently, you all too often make a big point of telling her you don't want anything to do with her." She tilts her head on one side and forces me to look into her eyes. "You shut her out, Jo."

I open my mouth to protest, but before I can speak Mum is talking again. "I'm not taking Amy's side, my darling. I'd just like you to see the . . . layers of the situation. That you haven't behaved perfectly yourself; that you above all her sisters should have some idea of what it feels like to have an impulsive personality and a hot temper; that I am making sure Amy is punished for what she has done, but the punishment should fit the crime. I've grounded her for a month and I've stopped her allowance." She squeezes my arm. "Please speak to her."

A knock at the door. I grab my tartan cap and shove it roughly on my head. "If you ask me, those punishments aren't enough," I mutter darkly. And then I turn and hurry outside to join Lateef.

It's good to be out of the house and even better to be with Lateef. We might have only known each other for a couple of weeks, but it already feels like ten times as long. All the tension I've been feeling in the house for the past few days ebbs away as we saunter towards the centre of Ringstone. I don't mention either the quarrel with Amy or Mum's attempt to get me to make up with her, and if Lateef guesses something is wrong he doesn't pester me to talk about it.

Instead we chat about the start of school tomorrow. I know, from the visit my sisters and I made to Ringstone Academy a month ago, that each year group has four classes, though certain subjects like maths and English are in sets for ability. Much to my delight I'm going to be in the same form as Lateef – and several friends of his whom I've already met and liked.

"So the only teacher to really watch out for is Mr Lymington." Lateef chats merrily away as we turn on to the High Street. The light is fading, a bank of grey clouds partially covering the weak sun. The shops are still open, their windows full of colourful clothes and food displays. "Mr Lymington's one of those teachers who turn suddenly, like you *think* they're happy for a bit of banter, then they get all cross out of nowhere."

"Teachers like that are a nightmare," I agree. I glance along the road. The Bookbound bookshop is just a few doors away, its dark red awning fluttering in the late afternoon breeze. In a few minutes I'm going to meet my hero, Rowena Riddell. My stomach tightens with excitement. "So, now you've seen the films, are you going read any of the *Blacktower* books?"

"Nah," Lateef says with a grin.

"But—"

"I'm in the bottom set for English, you know," Lateef goes on. "So that's one class we won't be together in."

I fall silent. Lateef is probably right. I've always done well in English lessons, though I don't want to say I'm expecting to be in the top set at Ringstone Academy in case it sounds boastful.

Bookbound is heaving with people. The queue is spilling out on to the pavement as we arrive. We stand waiting near the door, the winter sun so low in the sky that it glares off the windows. Most of the people here are our age or younger, though there's a sprinkling of older men and women too. The line moves faster than I'm expecting and soon we're inside the shop where the queue snakes around a large bookcase to where Rowena Riddell is, presumably, sitting at the back of the store.

Lateef chatters on with more gossip about school and the teachers and which people in our class are cool and which to be wary of. I'm not really listening as I crane my neck, trying to get a peek at my favourite author. Though the wait outside the shop seemed very short, the one inside goes on *for ever.* Well, it probably lasts about fifteen minutes, but I'm too impatient to just stand and talk to Lateef or even to check out the books on the shelves that we're passing.

At last we round the end of the big bookcase and Rowena Riddell appears in person. She's smaller and older than in her picture. From that I'd thought she was in her twenties, but this woman is at least as old as Mum. Possibly older. There are lines around her eyes, mouth and neck, and her hair is cut short with a lot of grey mixed in with the brown. She is wearing a blue jumper and lots of liner around her eyes, and both make her eyes look startlingly blue. She glances up at the queue every now and then and I imagine she's seeing me; seeing into me with those sharp eyes; seeing that I'm a kindred spirit, that I love her books, that I too am destined to be a writer.

Long stacks of the new book line the route to the desk. I take one and count out the cash I've been saving up. I pay the shop assistant when I reach the till and flick the book open. But I'm too excited to read. I clutch the book tight, my palms sweating on the cover.

We're next in the queue now. I'm vaguely aware of Lateef chatting away about something, but I'm too distracted to listen. Rowena Riddell is smiling at the girl in front of me. Soon she'll be smiling at me. I had a headful of stuff I was going to say to her, but now I can't remember a word of it.

"So, what do you think?" Lateef's voice pulls me back to reality.

I turn to him, distracted. "Think about what?" I ask.

He stares at me. "Jeez, Jo, weren't you listening to anything I said?"

Just then a crisp voice calls out: "Do you have a book for me to sign?"

Chapter 11

I spin around. Rowena Riddell – the author I have loved for so many years – is looking up at me from her signing desk. Her bright blue eyes are set deep in her face, their expression both frustrated and enquiring, like a bird might look if you were in the way of its dinner.

"Here's my book," I gush, thrusting it towards her. "I'm your biggest fan. I love your writing."

Rowena takes the book, still holding my gaze. She smiles, and the skin around her eyes crinkles.

"Thank you," she says. "That's lovely to hear. Which of my books have you read?"

"All of them," I gabble on. I've entirely forgotten that Lateef is here until he speaks.

"It's true," he says, folding his arms. "Jo reads, like, *all* the time, especially your books. And she's a writer too."

I cast him a warning glance.

"That's great," Rowena Riddell says. "So, shall I sign the book to you, Jo?"

"Yes, please," I say.

There's a short pause as she bends over my book, her pen gliding over the paper. My heart thuds. In a minute I'll have to make way for the next adoring fan. If I want to say anything important to her, it has to be now.

"I really do want to be a writer," I blurt out. "You and your books have inspired me and . . . and I was wondering if you had any advice?"

Rowena Riddell flicks her gaze up at me again. She tilts her head to one side, looking more like a bird than ever.

"Keep reading," she says eventually. "And keep writing. Don't give up." She hands me my book back. "It's always good to find a way of writing what you know." She grimaces. "A cliché, but true nonetheless."

I think about that. It's an odd thing for a fantasy writer to say – has Rowena Riddell ever fought off dragons or saved the world? I store the comment away to mull over another time.

"May I have a photo, please?" I ask.

"Sure."

I lean in and Lateef takes the pic.

"Good luck," Rowena Riddell says with a smile. "And remember, talent is all very well, but working hard is the most important thing. Most of success is just plain old graft."

"Thank you, thank you." I back away, then turn and hurry out of the shop. Lateef follows close behind.

I realize I've been holding my breath as the cold air whips around my head, and I take a deep, burning lungful. Out in the High Street the lamps have all come on, casting a soft light across the twilit pavement. Lateef says something but I can't hear over the traffic noise and the jubilant hum rising through my chest and throat, ringing in my ears.

"Wasn't she amazing?" I ask Lateef. It feels like my whole body is glowing with delight. "Wasn't that just the most brilliant experience *ever*?"

He laughs. "Definitely up there."

"I can't go back home, not straight away," I say. "I know! Let's go to the beach. I want to feel the sea breeze on my face, proper fresh air to be inspired by. The promise of strange and wonderful lands across the water. Not all these traffic fumes."

"But the beach is over a mile away," Lateef protests. "And it's winter!"

"So what? If I'm home by eight, Mum won't mind."

"OK. Sure." Lateef's eyes brighten. "How about Dead Man's Cove? You'll love it. Masses of atmosphere. It's dead spooky at night."

"Perfect," I say with a grin. "Rowena Riddell's inspired me to start a new story and a deserted beach sounds the perfect place to set it. I'm thinking historical . . . maybe something with smugglers who shipwreck boats and . . . and the daughter of a poor boatman who risks her life to save a young sailor who turns out to be the son of a wealthy lord. . ."

"Where on earth do you get all your ideas from?" Lateef asks, as we set off at a brisk walk.

"Dunno," I say. "Sometimes they just bubble up, like a bottle of fizzy drink when you shake it. And it only takes one thing to open the bottle and all the ideas froth out."

As we stroll along I think about what Rowena Riddell said: *Keep writing. Don't give up.* It's as if she *knew* Amy had destroyed my story and was telling me to keep writing, to persevere with my ambitions. And now I have an idea.

I talk through my smugglers story, and Lateef nods and whistles as the tale gets more and more dramatic. As we head away from the centre of town the streetlights disappear and the evening darkness surrounds us. Soon we're on the main road out of Ringstone. It's a very busy street with a narrow pavement on one side only and cars whooshing past at top speed, their headlamps flashing over the fields on either side. Lateef says he knows a shortcut to the beach across a field, so after ten minutes or so we turn off the road. Lateef opens the torch app on his mobile to light our way across the grass.

As we walk on I get a creeping sense that we're being watched. I can't explain it, but as I turn around and look over my shoulder, back at the main road, I catch sight of a figure hesitating at the intersection of the road and the field.

I peer through the gloom. I can't see her face in any detail, but it's a girl, quite slight, in a jacket with a thick scarf wound around her neck. There's something familiar about the shape of the head and halo of curls – and the way her chin sticks out is unmistakable.

"Amy!" I growl. What on earth is she doing here?

"Shall we let her catch up with us?" Lateef asks.

He still doesn't know about Amy destroying my story. I was going to tell him tonight, after the signing, but something holds me back. Lateef is so friendly and he has a way of seeing the good in everyone – he'd probably be as keen for me to make up with Amy as Mum is.

"No," I say. "She's been bugging me all week. Let's keep going."

I set off, walking quickly across the field. Lateef follows more slowly, looking back over his shoulder.

"What's Amy done?" he asks.

I say nothing.

"Shouldn't we at least make sure she's all right?" he asks. "Help her get home OK?"

A pang of guilt throbs through me. Maybe Lateef's right. It's dark and I'll bet Mum doesn't even know Amy's out – she's too young to be wandering around on her own. On the other hand, it's not my fault Amy followed me. She ruined my book and now she wants to spoil my trip to the beach.

No. She'll just have to look after herself. I grit my teeth and keep going.

A few minutes later we're on the other side of the field. "Where's the beach?"

"Just down that road." Lateef points into the darkness beyond.

We reach the trees that mark the start of the short beach. The sea is a black blanket, surrounded by the twinkling lights of the towns on either side of the bay. I can see what Lateef meant about it being spooky here – I feel like we've stepped back in time and a smuggler's ship might emerge from the mist. Annoyingly, though, I can't quite enjoy it. I'm cold and grumpy. All Rowena Riddell's inspiring words seem to have seeped away into the night.

Lateef is shining the light from his phone up and down the road, looking worried.

"We've lost Amy," he says.

"We didn't lose her," I snap. "She was never *with* us."

"I know, but—"

A high-pitched scream – a girl's scream – sears through the cold air. A second later a car whooshes past us at top speed. My heart lurches into my mouth as I spin around. Was that Amy screaming? Was she hit by that car?

I hesitate for a split second, straining to see up the road. But it's pitch black and silent.

"Oh God." Lateef's breathless whisper echoes the fear in my own heart.

"Amy?" I yell, breaking into a run. "*Amy?*"

The moon emerges as I charge down the street, looking frantically on either side. Lateef pounds along beside me.

Guilt swirls with panic, firing my feet across the tarmac. I can see Amy in my mind's eye, spread-eagled on the road, blood seeping from her lifeless body.

"Amy?" I shriek.

"Amy?" Lateef shouts.

It's only taken seconds but it feels like an eternity. The sound of sobbing echoes out from the trees to the side of the road.

"There!" Lateef points, the light from his phone shaking as he runs.

I strain my gaze, desperate. At last I see her. She's crouched over, leaning against a tree, crying like her heart would break. Her left side is covered in dirt where she must have fallen. I push myself to reach her, forcing the chill air into my lungs.

"Amy!"

She eases herself up. "Jo?" Her mouth wobbles and more tears flood out.

I pull her towards me. One of her sleeves is torn, her hands covered in mud. I hold her close. My sister, my stubborn, irritating little sister, is safe. "Are you all right? Did the car hit you?"

"No." She gulps back her sobs. "No, it almost did. I. . . I was too near the road, but no. . ." She looks up at me piteously and in her eyes I see nothing but remorse. "Oh, Jo, I'm so, *so* sorry I upset you. I'd give anything to take back what I did."

I glance around. Lateef is hanging back, watching us under the moonlight. I turn to Amy and in that moment I realize that what Mum said was true: no story is worth losing a sister over. Nothing is.

"I'm sorry that . . . that I was mean," I say, gruffly. "I should have forgiven you. And I should have tried to include you more in the first place."

Amy gazes at me, mud clumping her hair, her tears tracing lines through the dirt on her face. "So *do* you forgive me?" She hiccups, wiping her nose on her sleeve.

And in that moment my bitterness and anger fade away.

"Yes," I say, hugging her to me. "Of course I do. Though you're still the most annoying person on the planet."

"You too," she says, managing a small smile as she hugs me back.

We stand there and for a brief second I imagine what it would have been like if the car had knocked her over. I imagine Amy crumpled on the ground, and having to tell Mum and Meg and Beth. And Dad. I shiver and hold her even tighter. And then Lateef wanders over.

"Any chance we can get back home now?" he says with a grin.

"Absolutely," I say. "Let's go."

And we trudge back along the dark streets, across the field and through the centre of Ringstone. Lateef leaves us at his house and, my arm around Amy's shoulders, we cross Fishtail Lane and go home to Mum and our sisters.

Part Two

Spring

Chapter 1

School starts and, much to our relief, it isn't too bad. I was most worried about Beth but in fact she's had the least trouble settling in. It helps that it's a small school, though Lateef – who, unsurprisingly, is popular with everyone – has got his friends to make sure that their younger siblings in Beth's year are looking after her.

Lateef offered to do the same for Amy but, as I told him, Amy can look after herself. We're getting on better now, Amy and me. She still annoys me, but she doesn't push it so far any more and I'm trying to be nicer to her too. And I'm backing up everything I write on a memory stick, as well as online.

I do keep the memory stick safely hidden though, just in case.

I didn't go back to my Rodriguo and Rachel story. I thought about attempting a rewrite for a bit, but I couldn't get enthusiastic about starting all over again. Anyway, Rowena Riddell's advice to "keep writing" and not to give up at the book signing inspired me to try something new. So now I'm writing a fresh story. A series, in fact, called *The Tallulah Templeton Mysteries*.

Tallulah Templeton is me – or, rather, the me I'd like to be: she's smart and sassy, always able to say and do the stuff that I only think of after the moment is over! Tallulah is the kind of cool girl that everyone gravitates to, like she's got friendship magnets. Best of all, Tallulah has no sisters!

I've set up a blog and every couple of weeks I post a story in which Tallulah investigates missing stuff . . . a classmate's phone vanishes from her school bag and Tallulah finds out where she lost it, a friend's younger sister runs away from home and Tallulah works out where she's hiding.

It's the first week of March and I'm sitting at our kitchen table, putting the finishing touches to my most recent adventure. Tallulah is investigating the disappearance of her next-door neighbour's pet parrot, which has tried to fly home to the Caribbean but only got as far as Sidcup.

"Hey, Jo!"

I look up. Lateef is standing in the doorway. Beth, the long, red scarf she's been knitting dangling from her hand, hovers beside him. Mum has taken Meg and Amy window shopping – even though we have no money they still enjoy looking at the clothes.

"Hi," I say, glancing back at the screen. I'm in no mood to stop writing: Tallulah has just found out that her neighbour's parrot is hanging out at a tropical-themed adventure park called Island Paradise and has got stuck inside a ride called the Death Rattle. Tallulah is attempting to clamber through the empty carriages to reach the bird. It's dark inside the ride but outside the park is about to open and if Tallulah doesn't reach the parrot in time both she and the bird could be crushed under the wheels of the Death Rattle.

"Didn't you hear me calling your phone?" Lateef asks cheerfully.

"It's on silent while I'm writing," I say. "I'm in the middle of a Tallulah adventure."

"Again?" Lateef rolls his eyes in mock exasperation. He turns to Beth. "Never mind. Perhaps, while I'm waiting for Jo March, famous novelist, you might help me with one of my piano pieces? There's a place I always make a mistake; do you think you could show me where I'm going wrong?"

"Sure," Beth says, her eyes lighting up. "But I've only got our old keyboard. It won't sound as good as the piano in your house."

Lateef grins. "Wherever I play won't sound good anyway."

"Oh, Lateef, you're better than you think you are," Beth says very seriously. She sets down her knitting and they disappear into the living room.

I smile to myself. I'm fairly certain Lateef has no interest in improving his piano playing – he's just, in his typical way, trying to make Beth feel useful. And to encourage her to play in front of him, which she's still shy of doing.

A few minutes later I hear first what must be Lateef, slowly stomping out the notes of a tune, then Beth playing the same melody far more fluently.

I get Tallulah to the top of the Death Rattle just as the front door bangs open and Meg's voice echoes along the hallway.

"But the colour was all wrong," she's insisting.

"*I* liked the pink," Amy counters.

"Put the kettle on, one of you." That's Mum. She

sounds tired.

"I'll do it." That's Lateef. He must have gone out into the hall to say hello. I listen as Amy and Meg and Mum greet him. Lateef might be my friend more than anyone else's, but it's obvious from the warmth in their voices how pleased they all are to come home and find him here.

Seconds later, Meg and Lateef stroll into the kitchen. Lateef heads straight to the kettle while Meg flops into the chair opposite me.

"I bumped into Sallie Gardiner at the shopping centre," she says, eyes wide with excitement. "Guess what she told me?"

Sighing, I stop writing. Sometimes it's hard living with so many people in such a small house. I guess it's a bit like being permanently in a room with all the lights blazing, forcing you to live, constantly, in a blinding glare. I love my family, I really do, but not for the first time I find myself wishing I had more time to myself.

"Aren't you going to guess?" Meg persists. "It's *massive*."

Across the room, Lateef is fetching our big teapot, while the kettle hisses its intention to boil.

"Sallie Gardiner? Massive news?" I shrug. "I

dunno. Is she giving up shopping for the rest of the year?"

Across the room Lateef suppresses a laugh.

"No." Meg looks appalled. "Why would you even—?"

"I was joking." I make a face at her. "So go on, what is it then?"

"Her dad's friends with the Manning Plains Festival organizer," Meg gabbles, full of excitement. "He can get half-price tickets. I couldn't wait to tell you."

"Really?" I sit up. Manning Plains is the summer's hottest festival as far as I'm concerned. Not the biggest, of course, but the one where most of the bands Lateef and I like best will be playing. "How much?"

Meg makes a face. "That's the drawback," she says. "Even with the discount it's still nearly a hundred pounds for the weekend."

"Oh." I slump back in my chair. That's over half the money I've saved towards a new laptop. I can't afford the ticket. And I can't ask Mum. She never complains, but we're all aware she's got nothing to spare at the moment, that we're only just getting by.

I glance over to where Lateef is fetching mugs from

the cupboard, his back turned. I don't want him to realize how broke we are. "Never mind," I say.

Meg chatters on for a bit about what she'd do if *she* had a spare hundred pounds.

"I'm not really interested in Manning Plains," she says. "I'd rather spend the money on clothes. Mrs Gardiner's asked me to babysit the twins next week. She says if it goes well I can look after them over Easter too. Think how much I'll be able to earn."

I save what I've written to my memory stick then close my laptop and take them both upstairs. I stash them under my mattress, then wander into Mum's bedroom. One side of the bed is ruckled up with the duvet crumpled and the pillow at an angle. The other side – where Dad should be sleeping – is neatly smoothed down. It seems weird that he hasn't even seen this house. His last visit was back in October, when we were living in our old place. And now it's March and almost the end of our first term at school. I experience a throb of anger – if Dad worked at some ordinary nine to five job then not only would he be here, with us, but maybe we'd be able to afford me going to Manning Plains this summer.

As soon as I've had the thought I shake it off,

feeling ashamed of myself. Mum and Dad do the best they can.

I go to the bathroom and splash some water on my face, then head downstairs to hang out with Lateef.

He meets me halfway down the steps, eyes shining with glee.

"Come here," he says, grabbing my arm and dragging me back upstairs.

"What is it?" I ask.

Lateef's grin splits his face. "Brilliant news. As soon as I heard about Manning Plains, I called Uncle Jim. I said I wanted to use my birthday money to buy tickets – Sallie's dad's discounted tickets."

I stare at him.

"And he said yes, so I called Sallie and she's agreed I can have two, so I've bought them." He pauses for breath. "We can go, do you see, Jo? We'll be able to go to the festival. Together."

"You *bought* two tickets?" My head spins. I can't imagine being able to pick up the phone and spend nearly two hundred pounds. "Er, that was fast, Meg only just said."

"When I want something, I just go out and get it," Lateef says. "And I want nothing more than to go to that festival with you, Jo."

Emotions swirl inside me. On the one hand I'm thrilled at the prospect of being able to go to Manning Plains after all. On the other . . . I can't put my finger on why, but somehow it feels wrong. It's not just that it's too big a gift from Lateef, but also the way he's just decided for me, just bulldozed across my feelings, assumed that I need his . . . his charity."

"I can't accept the ticket," I say stiffly. "It's too much."

"What?" Lateef's face falls. "What do you mean?"

I don't know what to say. I don't really understand what it is I'm feeling, just that, for some reason, I'm angry at him. "You should have asked," I say at last.

Lateef stares at me across the landing, clearly bewildered. "*Ask*? But . . . but . . . are you telling me you *don't* want to go?"

"Of course I do," I snap. "I meant you should have asked if I mind you spending all that money on me."

"But it's my birthday money and . . . and it's a present." A look of utter bemusement fills his face

"A present I can't possibly ever match." My face feels hot, my stomach is churning. I thought Lateef understood everything about me.

Why doesn't he see that he's stomping all over my feelings?

"I don't care how much money you have or . . . or don't have," Lateef protests.

"Well *I* do." Fury whirls inside me. "You can't buy my friendship."

"How *dare* you say that's what I'm doing?" Lateef's voice is low, trembling with rage. I realize this is the first time I've ever seen him truly angry. His lips press together in a thin, tight line.

There's a long, horrible pause.

"I can't believe you're being so stupid about this," Lateef says at last, his voice oozing with bitterness.

"I'm not the one who's being stupid." My heart thuds. I'm desperately searching for a way of explaining how I'm feeling in a way that he'll understand.

Steps sound from below. Out of the corner of my eye I catch sight of Meg coming up the stairs. Lateef hears her footsteps too. "I'd better go," he says.

"Fine," I say coldly. I fold my arms.

Lateef gives me a final, furious look, then turns and hurtles down the stairs, pushing past Meg with an uncharacteristically curt "goodbye".

He disappears along the hallway. Meg turns, looks up at me. "What on earth was—?"

But I don't hear the end of her question. I'm already racing into my room, slamming the door behind me and hurling myself on to my bed, tears blinding my eyes.

Chapter 2

I weep into my pillow. Across the room I hear the door creak open. I grit my teeth, trying to stop my tears. Who the hell is that? All I want is a bit of privacy, some peace and quiet for myself. Back in our last house we each had our own room. Here it's impossible to ever get away. The only place I ever feel able to breathe is Lateef's house. And now. . .

And then, for a split second, my heart leaps with hope; has Lateef come back to apologize?

I look around. Meg is standing in the doorway.

My heart sinks again and I look away.

"What happened?" Meg asks. "Why is Lateef so cross?"

"I have no idea."

And I don't. All I did was point out he shouldn't have bought the tickets without asking me first. Why did he have to take that so personally? It's not my fault he was tactless.

You did accuse him of trying to buy your friendship, says a tiny, disapproving voice inside my head.

An image of Lateef's face, flushed and bewildered, flashes in front of my mind's eye. Losing his friendship feels like the end of the world.

I bury my face in the pillow again and sob bitter tears.

"Jo?" Meg shakes my shoulder. "Tell me what happened."

I sit up against the pillows and, with a deep sigh, tell my sister everything.

Meg nods and clucks sympathetically as I finish my tale.

"I can see it from both sides to be honest," she says thoughtfully. "I mean, I guess from Lateef's point of view he was just trying to do a nice thing for you."

"He should have asked me first," I say stubbornly.

Meg wrinkles her nose, like she does when she's thinking. "Why? I mean, why would that make it any better? It would still just be him maybe being a bit thoughtless but trying to do something nice, only without the surprise." She glances up at the pictures of Notre Dame and the Grand Canyon pinned above my bed. "He knows you want to travel, to try out new things; he's just trying to give you an . . . an adventure."

I shake my head. "He's obviously forgotten how humiliating it is to be paid for 'cos you can't afford something."

"Maybe not," Meg acknowledges. "Still, I'm sure you can make it up with him. Maybe leave it today, talk to him at school tomorrow?"

"I guess." I wipe my eyes, feeling a little better. "So did you buy anything at the shops?"

"This." Meg holds up a lacy top I hadn't even noticed was in her hands. "What do you think? It was, like, next to nothing in the sale. I reckon the colour will work really well with my grey cut-offs."

"You're so good at that stuff," I say, meaning it, but also wanting to offer my sister something nice as a thank you for her sympathy over Lateef.

"D'you really think so?" Meg beams. "Hey, look at this." She pulls out her phone, scrolls down the screen and hands it to me.

Dreams Dress Design, Ringstone. Summer Intern wanted.

I read on. It's a holiday job starting in a few months' time to cover the whole summer off school, from mid-July to early September. Apart from the fact that the job is unpaid, it would surely be perfect for Meg.

"Are you going to go for it?" I ask, looking up at her.

Meg shakes her head. "Nah, I'd never get it. It's not really my thing anyway. I just think it's really cool that *Dreams* has an office in Ringstone."

"Right." My mind goes into overdrive as I imagine how Meg would feel if she *did* get the internship. I'm sure she's only saying she doesn't want the job because she doesn't feel confident in her ability to impress a bunch of professional designers.

Meg burbles on about some dress she's seen, but I'm not really listening. She might not believe in her design talents, but I do. I wish there was a way of helping her see how creative she really is.

My mind drifts to Lateef again. Meg is right about leaving things for today and trying to make up with him tomorrow. The Easter break starts in a couple of weeks and Lateef and I had planned to spend the entire time hanging out together.

I don't want to miss all of that.

I don't want to miss Lateef.

I decide then and there to find him as soon as possible at school tomorrow morning, and explain why I was upset and that I didn't mean to seem ungrateful, I just don't want to be his charity case.

We can be friends again, I'm sure of it.

It doesn't even occur to me that I might be wrong about this.

The next day I'm walking through the playground, looking around for Lateef. I'm dawdling a little. Meg and Beth have already disappeared inside, leaving me with Amy, who for some reason is also in no rush to get into school. I spot him at last – he's on his own for once, looking for something in his school bag. It's the perfect opportunity to talk to him. I hurry over.

"Hey."

Lateef glances up, briefly, then looks back at his bag.

"Can we talk?" I ask.

"What about?" Lateef doesn't meet my eyes. "How you think I'm so desperate I want to buy your friendship?"

I suck in my breath. "I *don't*. Lateef, please, I *don't* think that. I—"

But Lateef is already walking away. I stare after him.

"Wow, he's really upset." Amy walks up.

"Yeah," I say with a sigh. "He's so angry with me."

Amy purses her lips. "I don't know that he looked angry," she says thoughtfully.

I glance at her.

"I'd say," she carries on, "he looked more hurt."

Is that true?

A crowd of year sevens rush past us, storming into the school, their voices turned up to high volume. The doors shut behind them and silence falls. It's a fresh, bright morning. The sun glints off Amy's golden hair.

"Lateef isn't hurt," I say, genuinely bemused. "You didn't hear what he said. He's angry, talking nonsense, because I didn't like the way he swooped in with his money and—"

"He thinks you don't like *him* any more." Amy stares at me, her sharp blue eyes sparkling. "Which destroys him because he likes *you*, you idiot."

She rolls her eyes in that spectacularly annoying way of hers, then stalks off inside the school building. I gaze after her.

She's got it all wrong. Lateef and I are just friends – good friends. The best. He doesn't *like* me – not in that way.

I'm sure of it.

Chapter 3

Another two weeks go by, the end of term passes and still Lateef keeps his distance. Meg's out every day, busy babysitting the little Gardiner boys. She comes home every afternoon full of stories about the arts and crafts they did together or how they played ball in the park. It sounds boring to me, but Meg seems super happy. Certainly a lot happier than I am. Without Lateef, I'm more miserable than I have been for ages, so I throw myself into a new Tallulah mystery, writing non-stop all day and most of the evening on the first Wednesday.

It's Beth's birthday on Friday – we're having a tea party. Just family – Beth doesn't want a big fuss. Normally Beth bakes all our birthday cakes. I decide this year I'll make one for her. I'll make a three-tier chocolate sponge with proper buttercream icing. It will be good to focus on something outside of my own troubles, as well as a nice thing to do for my sister.

Early on Thursday afternoon, when Beth is over the road, playing Uncle Jim's piano, I set to work. First step is to shoo Amy out of the kitchen. She disappears without any complaint, which strikes me at the time as odd, though I'm soon distracted fetching the flour, butter, sugar and eggs and weighing what I need in mum's old scales. I add a few heaped spoons of cocoa powder and mix everything together with the hand beaters. We used to have a proper mixer but Amy dropped it last year when she saw a spider and Mum can't afford to replace it just yet.

I pop the mixture into three tins and shove them in the oven, feeling very pleased with myself.

Twenty minutes later and I'm not so happy as I remove the cake tins and discover all my sponges are flat as pancakes.

"Could you have made more mess, Jo?" Meg says drily, wandering into the kitchen.

I look up. The kitchen *is* in a bit of a state. Eggshells are littered across the countertop, there's an expansive sprinkling of sugar on the floor by the sink and the self-raising flour bag has tipped over and cascaded half its contents over the baking trays which I pulled out of the cupboard earlier, didn't use and forgot to put back.

"My cakes haven't risen," I say mournfully.

"You probably didn't let the butter and the eggs come to room temperature before you used them," Meg says.

I stare at her. "How do you know to do that?"

"*Bake Off*," she says with a grin. "It's pretty basic stuff actually."

"Right." I sigh. "Well I'm going to have to start again."

"I'll help," Meg says. And the two of us set about creating another cake. This one is smaller – there isn't much butter left, but thanks to the fact I haven't put anything away, at least all the ingredients are at room temperature.

The kitchen looks like a tornado has hit it after we've finished – Meg is no better at clearing up after herself than I am – but we do end up with two properly risen sponges.

"So have you applied for that summer intern job yet?" I ask, as we set the cakes on the wire cooling rack.

"Nah, I told you, I'd never get something like that," Meg says. "I'm hoping Mrs Gardiner will need me to babysit the twins over the summer anyway."

A few minutes later she skips off to meet some friends in the centre of Ringstone. I make a stab at clearing up but I'm not really concentrating as I wipe cake mixture off the countertop. I've just had the most brilliant idea... Why don't I apply for that internship on Meg's behalf?

I'm sure she'd love to do the job; it's just that she lacks the confidence to apply. And it will be a way of saying thank you for helping me with the cake.

I hurry upstairs, fetch my laptop and find the ad online.

I go to town on the application, writing – as Meg – a far more colourful description of her talents than I would dare to produce on my own behalf. I stress how ambitious I, Meg March, have always been to become a designer, how I'm always studying designs and sketching my own ideas. That last part is a bit of an exaggeration of course, but what the heck, I need to make Meg look as good as possible. I create a new email address using Meg's name and send off the application.

I pad downstairs to carry on clearing up in the

kitchen, and my thoughts drift to Lateef again – and how he won't speak to me. He might have come from extreme poverty, landing in Britain without either funds or family, but he's spent the past seven years with everything he could possibly want offered to him on a plate. He must have forgotten what it's like to be poor. There's no other explanation for him not understanding why I was upset.

I gaze around at the kitchen. A selection of cake tins plus the mixing bowl and what looks like every utensil from the cutlery drawer are still spread across every surface. I check the time. Mum will be home any second. I don't want her to walk in on all this mess.

"Amy, give me a hand, will you?" I call next door, where Amy is watching TV.

"I'm busy," she yells back.

"But Meg and I made the cake," I say, going over and standing in the doorway. "It's only fair you should clean up afterwards."

"Yeah, right." Amy sticks her chin in the air. "What did your last slave die of?"

"You are so annoying," I growl, stomping over to the huge pile of washing up.

I clear away most of the dirty pans then mix up

a bowl of buttercream icing. Beth is great at putting little swirls on cupcakes and I'm determined to make a lovely pattern on top of her cake, but as soon as I fill an icing bag and try to pipe out little swirls on the top, the cake shifts and all I create are splodges. I try everything: wedging the cake, piping with one hand.

It's a lot harder than it looks.

Mum returns about ten minutes later. "Oh dear," she says, looking at the messily iced cake.

"I know," I wail. "And I wanted it to be so nice for Beth."

Mum laughs. "Come on. Nothing we can't rectify." She takes the cake from me and with expert hands smooths flat the icing I've been struggling to apply. She takes the bag and pipes a few decorative rose shapes across the top, then hands me a tube of coloured sprinkles to scatter over them.

It's all done in about two minutes and with epic effect.

"That looks brilliant," I enthuse, hugging her. "Thanks, Mum."

She smiles. "Why don't you go over to see Lateef? Remind him about Beth's birthday tea?"

I shake my head, miserable suddenly at the mention of his name. I haven't talked to Mum about my bust-up with Lateef, but I'm certain Meg will have filled her in on the details.

"I tried to talk to him when we were still at school. He wouldn't listen."

"So? Try again," Mum says.

I frown, surprised at how emphatic she sounds.

"Why do you think he's so angry with you?" Mum asks.

"Because I said he should have asked before buying me a festival ticket."

"Well, I think perhaps he should," Mum says. "And you *both* should have asked me and Uncle Jim for permission. But is that really why he's angry?"

I shrug, feeling slightly wrong-footed.

"Did anything else happen?" Mum asks. "Did one of you . . . say something else?"

"Well. . ." I squirm. "I did accuse him of trying to buy my friendship with the ticket."

Mum sighs. "Do you really think that's what he was doing?"

"No," I admit. "I think that he was trying to do a nice thing for me using his birthday money, but he got a bit carried away and made it sound like he could get anything he wanted with his masses of money even though he knows I don't have any. . ." I stop, my face flushing as hurt and anger rise inside me again.

"So he was clumsy, maybe a bit tactless and definitely very impulsive." Mum tilts her head on one side. "Remind you of anyone, Jo?"

I meet her gaze. A few moments pass as I let what she's said sink in.

"Do you think I should have let him pay nearly a hundred pounds for a ticket for me?" I ask, feeling suddenly uncertain.

"No, absolutely not," Mum says. "But I also think that if he wants to spend his birthday money on a treat for you both there were better ways of reacting … perhaps you could have said you'd go halves on the ticket? I know you have money saved for a laptop. Perhaps you could contribute some of that?" She hesitates. "Either way, you need to consider how much Lateef's friendship matters to you. Whether or not you can find it in your heart to apologize for anything you may have said that was hurtful."

"Suppose he won't listen?"

"Then at least you'll have tried."

I hesitate a second, then look around the kitchen at the icing bags strewn across the worktop.

"Don't worry about clearing this up," Mum says. "I'll get Amy to help."

I can't help but grin at that. And I'm still grinning as I rush out of the house a few seconds later. Lateef has to listen to me now. Our friendship is too important for him not to.

Chapter 4

Uncle Jim lets me in before I've even knocked. I can hear Beth in the distance on the piano. Jim presses his finger to his lips. "I saw you from the window. Beth thinks I'm upstairs, not listening," he whispers. "It's the only way she'll play."

I nod. "Is Lateef in?" I whisper back.

Uncle Jim points upstairs and a moment later, I stand outside Lateef's bedroom door, knocking and getting no reply.

"Lateef, please let me in!" I call out, not caring if anyone downstairs hears me.

The bedroom door opens. Lateef is standing there. He isn't smiling. "Announce yourself to the entire world, why don't you," he mutters.

I hesitate for a second, then push my way past him into the room. "If you'd let me in sooner I wouldn't have had to shout," I snap.

"Have you been in a food fight?" Lateef asks.

I glance across the room to his mirror. Jeez, I look a state. Mixture from Beth's cake – I'm not sure which attempt – is daubed across my forehead and left cheek, while there are greasy butter stains all down my top.

"It's Beth's birthday tea tomorrow," I explain. "Remember?"

"Of course," Lateef says. He indicates a carefully wrapped package on his desk. "I was going to drop that off for her seeing as you probably don't want me to come any more."

I look away. Of course Lateef should be there. Beth would want that too. "I was making a cake for her. It was a nightmare."

"I bet." A smile twitches at his lips.

Silence falls. I gaze around Lateef's bedroom. As usual, it's crammed with gadgets: a PC, an Xbox and several sets of game controllers, a proper camera plus tripod, a line of model motorbikes under a row of identical posters and even a woodworking bench in the corner. There's a walk-in closet full of designer clothes, a big orange couch, a double bed with an orange cover and a bedside lamp with a football base and a tangerine-coloured lampshade.

"There's a lot of orange in here," I say, feeling slightly at a loss.

"I love orange. It's the colour of the dress my mum was wearing the last time I saw her."

"Oh."

Lateef pauses. "Why are you here, Jo?"

I take a deep breath. "OK . . . so . . . you're my best friend and I'm so sorry I upset you," I say. "I'd give anything to take back what I said about you trying to buy my friendship. That was mean and . . . and untrue. Obviously."

A moment passes. Another. I fix my gaze on Lateef's face. He stares back, a million expressions passing through his eyes.

"I was just shocked that . . . that you'd spent so much money. . ." I stammer. "But I'd love to go to Manning Plains, if you still want to. So long as you let me go halves on my ticket, because—"

"It's OK." Lateef cuts me off. "I'm sorry too. Uncle Jim said I was tactless. And he suggested going halves too, so . . . so. . ." He looks up. "I'm sorry if . . . that I . . . offended . . . upset you. . ."

"That's OK," I say.

There's an awkward pause. "So, er, Beth's birthday?" He clears his throat. "I got her this big knitting set from Aspen's . . . like wool and patterns and stuff. Do you think she'll like it?"

I gulp. "I'm sure she'll love it," I say. "Though to be honest, Beth never wants anything. Except. . ." I hesitate, meeting his gaze. "Except I'm sure she'd like it if you were friends with me again."

"Wouldn't that make her birthday all about you? Still, if it's what Beth wants. . ." Lateef says, the corner of his mouth lifting slightly. "Even if it means I have to eat your cake."

"I wouldn't make you do that." I grin. "There are limits even to friendship."

"So, have you seen that YouTube thing with the clown and the puppies?" Lateef asks.

"No" I say.

"Look." He reaches for his phone.

And, just that that, our friendship is back.

Beth loves her birthday cake. She also loves her presents: the fresh flowers and bath oils from Amy, the new top from Meg and the book from me. Lateef adds a jumbo bag of mixed sweets and chocolates – all

Beth's favourites – to his knitting-set gift, while Mum has lined up private piano lessons to go through the Easter and summer holidays. Though Beth is super appreciative about everything, you can tell that it's this last present that makes her the most happy.

Luckily, Aunt Em is away for work so she doesn't come, though she does send Beth a bunch of fat, white lilies. The formal arrangement of heavily perfumed blooms tied together with expensive-looking satin ribbon is about as far away from Beth's personality as a bunch of flowers could be, but Beth is characteristically sweet-natured about it.

"She's very sorry to miss out, Bethy," Mum explains. "She says that she'll be here for lunch on Easter Sunday."

"Great," I growl under my breath.

"It was very thoughtful of her to send the flowers," Beth says.

We have all eaten our cake and drunk several cups of tea when there's a knock on the front door.

Mum goes to answer it.

"Perhaps that's Aunt Em after all," suggests Meg.

Outside in the hall, Mum says, "Of course, bring it in. I'll call Beth." I can hear the smile in her voice.

"That's not Aunt Em," I say. "Come on."

The five of us crowd out into the hall where Mum is standing by the open front door.

"We'll just fetch the ramp, roll it in for you," says a male voice from outside.

"What on earth?" Beth scuttles forward. She sees whatever is outside and claps her hand over her mouth.

"What is it?" I ask, hurrying over.

"I can't see," complains Meg.

"Or me," says Amy.

Mum pushes the door open wide. I gasp. Uncle Jim's white piano stands outside. Unmistakable, even down to the little chip on the top.

"Ha!" Lateef says with a chuckle. "It's finally here! I've been dying to tell you. Uncle Jim made me swear to keep it a secret."

"Is it really for me?" Beth says in a whisper.

"It came with this," Mum says, handing her a card.

I watch over Beth's shoulder as her trembling fingers fumble with the envelope. She draws out a birthday card with a pencil sketch of a daisy on the front.

The message inside has been handwritten.

Beth reads, her fingers gripping the card so tightly her knuckles are white. She smiles faintly.

"What does it say?" Meg asks.

Beth pushes the card at me, tears bubbling into her eyes. "You read it, Jo," she says at last.

I clear my throat and read: *"Dear Beth. I have had many fine scarves in my life, but I never had one that suited me so well as yours."*

"The scarf you were knitting . . . that was for Uncle Jim?" I ask.

"Really?" Meg sounds astonished.

"You never said a word," Amy adds. She gives Beth a spontaneous hug. "You're so good."

"It was to say thank you for letting me use the piano," Beth explains. Mum strokes her hair.

"Go on, Jo, finish reading," Mum says.

"I like to pay my debts, so I hope you will allow me to send you something which once belonged to my daughter, Francesca. I'm sure both she and her mother would want you to have it as much as I do. With many thanks for your beautiful playing, Uncle Jim." I give Beth back the card. "That's amazing," I say.

Beth stares, open-mouthed, at the piano. Then she turns to Lateef.

"Are you sure you don't mind?" she asks timidly. "I mean, what are you going to practise on?"

"Uncle Jim's letting me give up piano at last, thank

goodness." Lateef laughs. "You are more welcome to the thing than I can tell you."

"Let's get this inside," says the man who spoke before, reappearing with a ramp. Lateef and I help the man push the piano into the house and along the hallway.

"It can go here," Mum says, pointing to the wall by the door in the living room. "That's a perfect spot for it."

The piano is soon set up. Beth, with little urging for once, sits and plays – Chopin I think. Meg stands next to her and turns the pages.

Mum stands back in the doorway, watching Beth play.

"Is it OK for us to keep the piano?" I ask her quietly. "I mean, it's a huge present. Much bigger than festival tickets."

"That's true." Mum murmurs. "But yes, I think under the circumstances it's right to keep it. Jim asked me beforehand, made sure I didn't mind." She smiles at me. "I can't deny that when he first suggested the gift I wanted to say no, just out of pride, but then I thought of the joy it would bring Beth. *And* Jim." Her eyes fill with sadness. "He told me he always wanted it to be used, but couldn't bear to be parted from something that had meant so much to his daughter. I think that's why he put poor Lateef under so much pressure to have lessons. I guess now he's met Beth he feels the piano will be going to a good home."

Beth stops playing. "What am I doing? I must go and thank Uncle Jim," she says, with uncharacteristic forcefulness. She stands up.

I exchange a look with Mum and Meg. Where did this new, confident Beth come from? The surprise on their faces echoes my own.

"Shall I come with you?" I offer.

"No thanks," Beth says firmly. "I'm just going to tell him that he's welcome to come and hear me play whenever he wants. No need for anyone else to bother themselves."

My jaw drops. Mum's and Meg's do too. And before anyone can say anything else, Beth is already out of the house and halfway across the road.

"What's got into her?" I turn to Mum.

Mum smiles. "I think," she says, "that our Beth is growing up."

Chapter 5

It's Saturday morning, the day after Beth's birthday. Beth herself is at home with Mum, playing on her new piano, while Amy is at a friend's house, working on her art project. Meg, meanwhile, is at the Gardiner's house, babysitting the twins while the rest of the family go to a wedding.

Lateef and I are hanging out at the shopping centre in Ringstone. We mooch along to the fountain in the central section of the mall. Lateef has a fascination with water in public places – he loves the swimming baths too. Right now he's standing, leaning on the surrounding railing, and gazing in wonder at the water cascading over the stone.

"Why do you like looking at it so much?" I ask.

"Dunno," he says with a shrug. "I never saw a fountain until I came here. I mean, there are plenty in Iraq, just not where I was from."

I study his eager face. It's easy for me to forget Lateef originally came from another country, far away. Most of the time he seems just like the rest of us.

"What d'you like about it?" I ask. The three-tier fountain seems an ugly thing to me, grey with green tinges at the edges of the stone, though the effect of the cascading water is pretty.

"The way it works," Lateef explains. "It's so simple and beautiful, the water spouting out of the top, then getting sucked up at the bottom to be reused."

His phone rings. Answering, Lateef snaps back into social mode, greeting the caller cheerfully. I turn away, surveying the Saturday morning crowds: there's an elderly couple walking slowly, both leaning on sticks, a young dad pushing a buggy past a knot of young teenage girls at the doughnut stand and a middle-aged woman chasing after a toddler who is shrieking with laughter as he trots away from her as fast as possible.

Watching the little boy gives me a new idea for a Tallulah Templeton story... Perhaps in her next adventure she could investigate a missing child, last seen in a local shopping centre. I stare into the distance in the direction of, but not really focusing on, the girls at the doughnut stand. They're a typical bunch of teenage girls – artfully tousled hair, fashionable clothes – and I can hear their bird-like chatter from here.

And then the smallest girl, standing on the edge of the group, moves into view.

It's my youngest sister.

"That's *Amy*," I say, blinking with surprise. "What's she doing here?"

"Where's she supposed to be?" Lateef asks, pocketing his phone.

"I don't know, but she said this morning she was at a friend's doing project work for her art class." I pause. The idea that she would have lied to me about what she was doing today gives me an uneasy feeling. Amy is stubborn and irritating, but she isn't a liar. She must have lied to Mum too. A far bigger crime.

"I thought Amy seemed really quiet yesterday," Lateef says thoughtfully. Then he says, "By the way, that was Tiny on the phone. He's going bowling. Do you want to come too?"

I'm focusing so much on Amy I barely hear him. She

was quiet yesterday. In fact, now I'm thinking about it, she's been quiet since we broke up from school two weeks ago. I peer more closely at the group of girls. I recognize a couple of them from the corridors at school – popular, confident girls with nice clothes.

As I watch, I realize that one of the group says something to Amy. Something about my sister's posture – head bowed, eyes downcast – doesn't look right to me. Amy usually has her chin in the air and doesn't fear anybody.

"So, d'you want to come with me, Jo?" Lateef prompts. "Or shall I see you later?"

"Later, thanks." I nod towards Amy. "I want to keep an eye on her."

Lateef leaves and I edge closer to Amy. I hate the idea of spying on her – but something here doesn't feel right. I creep over and hide behind the doughnut stand.

"It has to be two bottles or it doesn't count," one of the girls is saying. I peek out and recognize her from towards the end of term when she came home after school one day with Amy. Carla. She has masses of silky hair and is always perfectly dressed.

"Two bottles is easy." I know that tone in Amy's voice: defiant and trying to be tough.

"And not soft drinks," says another girl. "Obviously."

"I *know,*" Amy insists. "And spirits rather than wine. But wine will do. I *know.*"

Is she promising them alcohol? My jaw drops.

"Any questions?" Carla asks.

"So if I get it, I can definitely come to the party?" Amy's voice is slightly tremulous.

So that's it. I don't have it in me to be angry. In fact my heart goes out to her. Amy was in the cool gang at our old school. Now she is clearly trying to buy her way into a new clique with the same status here.

Carla says something in a low voice I can't hear, then she and her friends flounce off, giggling, leaving Amy alone. I hesitate. Every instinct I have tells me she'll hate the fact I've overheard the conversation she just had. But I have to do *something.*

"Hey." I walk around the stand.

Amy jumps, her eyes flashing up at me. She glances around nervously. "What are you doing here?"

"I was hanging with Lateef, but he's gone to meet Tiny. What about you?"

"Nothing," she says, shuffling from foot to foot, clearly scrambling to come up with a story. "That is, er . . . I'm meeting someone, a friend from school. We need stuff for the art project."

"Right." Maybe if I were Meg or Beth, Amy would volunteer information about what's just happened, but I guess she doesn't feel comfortable doing that with me. I can't really blame her – I've always been tough on Amy. But then, I've always thought she was tough herself. Which, I suddenly realize, she isn't at all.

"Look," I say, trying to sound more sympathetic. "I promise I wasn't stalking you but I saw you here with those girls and you looked miserable so I came over and. . ." I wait, hoping she'll confide in me. When she doesn't, I go on. "I couldn't help but overhear what you were saying. About trying to buy booze."

Amy's eyes widen in horror.

"I'm not judging you," I carry on quickly. "But. . . It's just. . ." I've leapt into this conversation too fast, I realize. I don't know what to say to her.

Amy stares at me, her mouth set in a defiant line. I can see that she'd rather die than have my pity. And in that moment it occurs to me that Mum is right – Amy and I are more alike than I've ever realized.

"You can't buy friends with alcohol," I say at last. "And, obviously, you can't buy alcohol either. And you can't steal it. So you're basically screwed every which way."

Amy hangs her head.

I try another tack.

"Are those really your friends?" I ask. She shrugs. "Because I don't think real friends would ask you to do something like this. I don't get it, Amy. You always say you're getting on well with everyone."

"I have to, don't I?" Amy spits, looking up at last. Tears bubble up in her eyes. "Everyone else is all so super happy with *their* classes and lessons and new friends." Her voice cracks. "Even Beth is doing fine and she can barely get a sentence out in front of strangers."

A tear trickles down her cheek. She wipes it away angrily.

I bite my lip. I had no idea Amy was lonely. "But you always make out like you're great, that you've settled in brilliantly." I hesitate. "Isn't there anyone you like at school? Not because they're cool – just because they're nice?"

"There's one girl, Katy Brown. She's asked me to her house a few times," Amy says. "I told Mum I was with her this morning. I like her. But I wanted to get in with the cool group."

"You mean those girls you were talking to?" I ask. "Like Carla?"

Amy nods. "She's having a party, Carla. Everyone important will go. I need to be there. That's what the drink is for."

"Listen, Amy," I say. "Girls like Carla aren't worth bothering with. She may be popular and cool or whatever, but it's not worth selling your soul to hang out with her. Or her friends."

Amy stares sulkily up at me.

"Don't you see?" I persist. "Those girls won't really like you, not if they think they can buy you. They'll always be getting you to run errands for them, like the alcohol thing." That point hits home. Amy looks thoughtful. If there's one way to get through to her, it's by appealing to her pride. "You don't want to be Carla's lapdog for the rest of your school life, do you?"

Amy shrugs. I sense I'm beginning to convince her.

"I think you should forget Carla and her party and buying your way to an invitation," I press on. "Send her a text right now, saying you're not playing her games any more. And I think you should call Katy and go round her house so you're not lying to Mum. I'll walk you over there if she's in. Deal?"

There's a long pause and then, very slowly, Amy nods. "Fine," she says with a sigh.

Together we compose a text for Carla – not as forthright as I originally wanted, but making it clear nonetheless that Amy won't be providing alcohol for her party. Amy presses send.

"Relieved?" I ask.

Amy shrugs. "Maybe. A little bit."

"Now call Katy," I order.

I wait with Amy while she makes the call. In typical Amy style, she is relaxed and friendly with Katy, quickly getting an invite to go over to her place. We walk there in silence, but when we reach the little brick house, just a few roads from our own, Amy says:

"Thanks for not running to Mum about the alcohol thing. And . . . and thanks for getting me out of Carla's party. You're right. I don't want to be anyone's lapdog."

I give her a little wave and watch her walk up the path.

I don't feel like going to meet Lateef and Tiny at the bowling alley, so I wander home. Meg is still out, so I settle down in our bedroom and open my laptop.

There's an alert from the email account I set up in

her name. I open it quickly and read the email from someone called Samantha Burns at Design Dreams.

Hi Meg, thanks so much for your application. We were so impressed by your ideas and commitment to a career in design and we'd love to invite you to come for interview with regards to the internship available in July.

"Yes!" I punch the air.

First I successfully talk Amy out of a life of crime and moral degeneracy. And now it seems I've launched Meg's fashion career.

Wait till I tell her. Meg is going to be thrilled.

Chapter 6

"You did *what?*" Meg's face pales under the electric light of the hallway. I've rushed downstairs to tell her the brilliant news. But she doesn't look pleased. In fact she looks appalled.

Mum and Beth appear.

"What's going on?" Mum asks.

"Jo has. . ." Meg shakes her head. "It's *unbelievable*, Mum. Jo has *impersonated* me and signed me up for a summer job that I didn't even *know* about." Her voice rises as she speaks.

"Jo?" Mum asks, a warning note in her voice. "Is this true?"

"It's an internship at a fashion company," I explain, desperate to make them see it's a brilliant opportunity for Meg. "They're called Design Dreams, they're famous. Meg *showed* the ad to me, she said she'd love it but she wouldn't get it so I—"

"I *never* said that," Meg shouts. "I told you several times that I didn't *want* that stupid job. I already *have* a job, looking after the Gardiners' little boys."

I shake my head. "But that's just babysitting. This would be perfect for helping you become a fashion designer."

Meg rolls her eyes. "For goodness' sake, Jo. I don't want to be a fashion designer."

"But—"

"You'll have to email them back and say there was a mistake and I don't want the job."

"It's not a job, it's a summer holiday internship," I say stubbornly.

"Oh, great," Meg's voice drips with sarcasm. "So it's not even paid."

She stomps off upstairs. I turn to go after her, but Mum puts her hand on my arm.

"Leave it, Jo," she says gently.

"I was only trying to help." I look at Beth, she's always on my side; surely she'll back me up? But Beth is gazing down at her shoes. "Meg should have more confidence in her abilities," I protest.

Mum sighs. "Her abilities for doing what? Have you ever actually seen Meg try to design anything? Has she ever told you she wants to be a designer?"

"I guess not in those words," I'm forced to admit. "But she'd be great at it. I mean, Meg *loves* fashion. She's always looking at clothes and stuff online and she puts outfits together really well. It's . . . it's her *life*. Like writing is mine."

A little smile hovers around Mum's lips. "Do you think that maybe because you feel so passionately about writing, you've assumed Meg feels the same about dress designing?"

"I'm sure Meg *wants* to be a designer," I say. "She just doesn't know it yet."

The rest of the week speeds by. Meg is still in a mood with me. She's out most days babysitting, then off with her own friends in the evening. I've written to Design Dreams to say that she won't be coming for an interview – "unavoidable change in circumstances" is how I put it. I still feel cross but, as Mum says, what Meg does for work has to be her choice. I try to talk to Meg a couple of times, to persuade her that being a designer would be really cool, but she refuses to listen.

Amy is out most of the week too, at Katy Brown's house. On the Thursday before Easter weekend, she trots off at lunchtime, announcing that she and Katy are going to the cinema, but she'll be back by five.

Mum nods, looking pleased. Amy's friendship with Katy has gone from strength to strength since the incident in the shopping centre and Amy has massively lightened up as a result. I've made her promise to tell me if she hears any more from those mean girls in her class but so far standing up to them seems to be working. I've told Lateef – in strict confidence – that we need to look out for her a bit more, and Lateef has promised to do what he can to make sure she's OK when the summer term starts.

Everyone's home in time for our Skype call with Dad at six.

I grab an apple and a cereal bar from the stash in the kitchen, then take my place on the long sofa next to Mum. Beth is already on Mum's other side.

The Skype call sound chimes out.

"Meg! Amy! Come on!" Mum calls, as the pair of them rush into the living room and crowd on to the sofa beside us.

Meg and I usually squish up together, but this evening she sits further along the sofa, next to Beth.

Clearly she's still annoyed with me. I don't have time to dwell on this, though, as seconds later the image of Dad fills the screen.

I can't help but smile at the sight of his familiar face: the thick eyebrows and high forehead. Of all of us, I think he looks most like Meg, only with a long, sloping nose. His eyes twinkle as he smiles out of the screen at us.

"Oh, sweetheart, you look thinner," Mum says. "Is the food terrible?"

"Nah, I'm eating well," Dad says, beaming. "How are all my girls?"

It's weird only seeing him like this every few weeks. It feels like seeing a stranger sometimes – though of course he isn't one and soon we're chatting away as normal, Dad asking what we've been doing and smiling, his dark eyes darting over each of us in turn. I get my chance to tell him about the stories I'm writing. Dad is encouraging, as ever, urging me to keep going, asking for the link to my new Tallulah stories so he can read them too. And then comes the best moment of all, when Dad says he has an announcement – that he'll be home this weekend, late on Easter Sunday, just three days away.

We all cheer, and even after we hang up the good

mood stays as Mum bustles around the kitchen, overseeing our dinner preparations. She's got three job interviews next week – and is confident she'll soon be offered a permanent position. So Dad coming home feels like the icing on the cake for us.

I look around at the excited faces, grinning. Things are going well, at last. I've got my friendship with Lateef, the excitement of my stories and a music festival ahead. OK, so Meg and I have fallen out, but she'll get over it sooner or later, and apart from that she seems well and happy. It strikes me that we're finally settling here in Ringstone. All at once I'm brimming with happiness, sure that from now on things can only get better.

I couldn't be more wrong.

Chapter 7

The next three days pass as normal. I don't try to talk to Meg about the design internship again and she doesn't mention it herself. She doesn't talk much at all, in fact, but least she doesn't seem quite so annoyed with me any more.

To be honest, everyone's so excited about Dad coming home there's hardly any time left to talk about anything else. The time until he gets here seems to stretch out like a piece of gum that gets further and further away as you pull on it. We all work on making the house and garden as nice as possible, tidying our rooms and weeding and pruning outside. Amy does a portrait of us all in charcoal and frames it, so that Dad can take it away with him when he leaves. Lateef brings us fresh flowers from his garden to fill the vases, so that the air is rich with scent. We all want his visit home to be perfect.

And then, finally, the day itself is here. Even though Dad's return this evening is the Main Event of the day, Mum insists that preparations for our usual Easter lunch with Aunt Em continue as planned. Meg helps her roast a leg of lamb and a tray of potatoes while Beth makes an apple tart for dessert. I'm in charge of prepping the green beans, a grubby head of cauliflower and some garden peas that Mum has bought at the local market, while Amy and Lateef – who's been allowed to come for lunch on condition he goes to a family function with Uncle Jim later – lay the table.

Aunt Em herself arrives at midday. It's teeming down outside and though, as usual, she's dressed to the nines in a cashmere coat with a fur collar, her usually sleek hair is a little ruffled.

"Josephine?" she barks as I let her into the hallway. "Do something with this umbrella, it's soaking."

I take the umbrella from her – black with a silver handle. It's barely damp.

"It can't have rained much on the way from your taxi to the front door," I'm unable to resist saying.

"No need for backchat." Aunt Em tuts, heading straight for the downstairs bathroom. She emerges a moment later with smooth hair and a fresh application of bright red lipstick. "That's better," she says, marching into the kitchen. "Hello, everyone."

"Hi, Aunt Em!" Meg glances up from the potato tray, her face flushed with the heat from the oven.

Mum hurries over to kiss her sister-in-law on the cheek. They couldn't look more different: Aunt Em is neat and thin, all cheekbones and hard angles, whereas there's a softness to Mum, in spite of her slimness and her height. Watching them together it strikes me that even though everyone says I look like Mum, I probably resemble Aunt Em more physically. I don't like the thought.

"Hello, Auntie," Amy says with a winning smile, coming in from the living room. "Would you like a drink?" She always seems to know the right thing to say to our formidable aunt.

"Indeed I would," Aunt Em says approvingly. "White wine, please, Amy. You'll find a chilled Sancerre in here." She passes Amy her capacious handbag. Meg's eyes linger on it longingly so presumably it's some sort of designer accessory, though I can't see an obvious label or logo.

"Hello, I'm Lateef. I live over the road." Lateef beams, offering his hand for Aunt Em to shake. "It's a pleasure to meet you."

Aunt Em eyes him thoughtfully. "Well, it's nice to meet you too, young man." She shakes his hand, then turns to Beth. "Are you not going to say hello to me, Elizabeth?"

Beth trots dutifully over and kisses Aunt Em on the cheek. She finds Aunt Em's abrasive manner terrifying.

"And how is your music coming along?" continues Aunt Em. When Beth murmurs that she's still practising daily, Aunt Em's delicate brows arch.

"Good, and perhaps you'll also practise not mumbling quite so much when you speak to me too." She grins, as if she's said something funny. Beth shrinks away. I glare at my aunt, who fixes me with a stern look. "That frown doesn't suit you, Josephine," she tuts. "And while I'm on the subject, your hair needs shaping into a proper style. A trim at least. It really could be your crowning glory, if you could be bothered with it."

"Maybe there are more important things in life than hair and—?" I begin.

"Lunch will be ready in about an hour," Mum

interrupts, throwing me a warning glance. "Jo, please would you open some crisps while Amy gets Aunt Em her drink? Lateef, do make yourself at home, dear."

Grudgingly I empty a bag of ready salted into a bowl and take it through to the living room where Meg is grilling Aunt Em about her handbag, which leads to an account of her recent business trip to Paris. Amy hovers attentively on Aunt Em's other side. Lateef is smiling and nodding, his usual charming self.

I plonk my bowl of crisps down, earning a brief look of scorn from Aunt Em, and retreat to the kitchen, where Mum is now basting the lamb, a sheen of sweat on her forehead, and Beth is carefully layering caramelized apple slices along the top of her tart.

"It can go straight in to heat up when you take the lamb out to rest," she's saying.

"Thanks, Bethy," says Mum, wiping her forehead. "I just want everything to be nice."

Beth turns to me. "Don't listen to Aunt Em, Jo," she says quietly. "I think your hair is lovely just the way it is, all long and wild."

I kiss her cheek, check that Mum doesn't need

help with anything, then slip away to my room and lose myself in a Tallulah Templeton mystery. Much more fun than making small talk with Aunt Em.

Lunch passes smoothly enough. Aunt Em does most of the talking, telling us more about her work trip to Paris.

"For once I made sure to leave enough time at the end of the trip to do some of the museums," she says with a smile. "The Louvre is just extraordinary."

"Did you make it to the Musée Marmottan ?" Amy asks. "That's where all the Monets are. We did about them at school."

"Oh I *love* the Impressionists" Aunt Em says, which sparks off a general conversation about the French artists and Monet in particular. To my surprise, Lateef joins in avidly – and knowledgeably; it turns out Uncle Jim took him to a big Monet exhibition in London a few years ago and he remembers several of the paintings really well.

I knew Lateef had travelled across Europe a lot with Uncle Jim, but I hadn't realized how many places he'd visited: he's been all over Spain and France and Italy. I listen with envy as he chats breezily away with Aunt Em about their respective trips.

Write what you know. Rowena Riddell's author advice pops into my head and I grimace. My life is so boring – I've only ever lived in a dull suburb on the outskirts of London and now here, in small-town Ringstone. We used to go on holiday to Devon, before Amy came along, but for the past few years we haven't even been able to afford that. I'd be embarrassed to admit it to anyone at school, but I've never even been abroad.

I tune back into the conversation, only to find the subject has moved on and that Meg is now holding court, making everyone laugh with her tale of little Tommy Gardiner's recent attempt at finger painting – and how his mother came home to discover bright blue handprints all over her favourite sofa.

I offer to clear away as soon as the apple tart has been eaten. Beth leaps up to help me. I'm hurrying, as usual, and manage to tip a glass of water into Aunt Em's lap. She jumps up as though scalded. Amy, thinking quicker than anyone else, grabs a clutch of paper napkins from the sideboard and falls to her knees, dabbing at Aunt Em's skirt. Lateef's eyes meet mine, sparkling with humour and I have to press my lips together, hard, to stop myself from laughing out loud.

"It's only water," Amy says, soothingly. "If we get the worst off I don't think the fabric will come to any harm."

I apologize quickly, then scurry away with my plates to start washing up. Lateef dries and Beth puts away. Once we've finished, Lateef gives a sigh and heads back to Uncle Jim's house in order to get ready for tonight's family function.

Not wanting to go back into the living room, Beth and I wander into the garden with mugs of tea. The earlier rain has stopped and the sun is shining. Beth sits in the only un-damp chair, under the awning, and looks out over the flowers that are just starting to spring up.

"I love this time of year," she says softly. "And I'm so glad the garden's looking nice for Dad to come back to." She grins. "Isn't it great, Jo? He'll be home in just a few more hours."

"I know," I say, smiling at her.

"I never imagined Ringstone would feel like home," Beth says thoughtfully, "but it does now, doesn't it?"

I nod. She's right; it does.

"So much has happened," she goes on dreamily. "Mum's got all those interviews next week and I'm sure at least one of them will lead to a job, and

Meg's really happy looking after the little Gardiner boys."

"And Amy's got friends," I add, "and I've got my stories and you have your new piano to play."

Beth sighs, bending down to pick up a crocus that's snapped off at the stem and is lying, alone, on the grass. "Sometimes I wonder if I'll ever do anything except play the piano. . ."

There's something odd in her voice – something sad – that makes me look up, but before I can ask, Mum calls from the kitchen.

"Girls!" She isn't shouting loudly, but something urgent in her voice sends a chill down my spine. I meet Beth's gaze and can see she's feeling the same.

We hurry inside.

Mum is leaning against the kitchen counter, her phone clutched tightly in her hand, her face the colour of pale ash.

"What's the matter?" Meg asks. She, Amy and Aunt Em have come in from the living room.

We all stare at Mum as she looks up at us, fear in her eyes. I've never seen her look scared before – not when Dad went away, not when she lost her job. Never. Mum is the strongest person I know – but now she looks as fragile as the crocus in Beth's hand.

"It's Dad," she says at last, her voice a whisper, and it's like all the air is sucked out of the room. "He's seriously ill. He . . . he collapsed just now, at the airport in Germany when he was waiting to change planes to . . . to come home. He's been taken to a local hospital in Frankfurt. That was the consultant on the phone. They've managed to stabilize him and they're running some tests tonight."

"Oh no!" Meg and Amy say in unison. Beth gasps, her hand flying to her mouth.

"What's the matter with him?" Aunt Em asks sharply.

She sounds cross and cold, like she so often does. I shoot her a warning look. This is not the time for harsh words. Can't she see how upset Mum is?

"They don't know yet." Mum's voice cracks. "Hopefully they'll have a better picture in the morning." She gulps. "They want me to fly out there straight away."

"Oh, Mum. . . Poor Dad." Our voices chorus. I can't bear the idea of him alone in a hospital, so far away.

"Can we go with you, Mum?" Beth asks. "Please, Mum."

"No, my darling," Mum says, touching her cheek gently. "The doctors say he's not well enough for visitors, even you four. I have to go on my own. I'll ring you as soon as I have any news at all, I promise." She looks at us each in turn, her forehead creasing with anxiety. "I hate to leave you."

"We'll be OK, Mum," I say stoutly. "Meg and I can keep an eye on the others."

"I don't need keeping an eye on," Amy whines. "You don't need to—"

"Oh no, I won't hear of you girls being on your own." Aunt Em's curt voice cuts in. "Obviously, I shall have to come and stay."

We turn and stare at her, open-mouthed.

"For as long as need be." She glances at Mum. "No need to worry about it."

"But Emmeline, I can't ask you to—" Mum stammers.

"You're not asking. I'm offering." Aunt Em says emphatically. "And if you remember, *I'm* the one who paid the landlord the deposit on this house, so I've as much right to be here as the rest of you."

"Of course." Mum blinks, clearly completely thrown. "I didn't mean to—"

"For pity's sake, do stop blathering on," Aunt Em interrupts. She turns to the rest of us. "Margaret, you help your mother pack. Josephine, research flights and book the first one out – if you can manage that. Here's my credit card. Amy, you can come with me and help me pack. Which leaves. . ." Her eyes light on Beth. "Elizabeth, perhaps you'd get your mother's room ready for me? And you can help her later, Josephine – if you're able to do it without damaging anything." She claps her hands together, clearly irritated by the fact that we're all still gazing at her in shock. "Come *on,* everyone. Let's go!"

We all jump into action. And just an hour later, around the time we'd have been expecting Dad to walk in the door, we find ourselves waving Mum off in her taxi with messages of love for Dad and deep anxiety in our hearts.

Aunt Em, who arrived back from her own house about half an hour ago accompanied by two of the largest suitcases I've ever seen, has already got me and Meg to haul them upstairs and is busy unpacking her things in Mum's room.

The rest of us huddle in the living room. The sky is darkening outside but nobody switches on a light. We all sit in shock. I know what the others are thinking. How can a day that started in one way, full of such hope and promise, finish so differently?

"I hope Mum's got everything she needs," muses

Meg, a little frown between her eyes that reminds me of Mum.

"I know. I packed a book for her to read in hospital," I add, thinking of the lonely hours she will spend waiting for news.

"I hope she remembered her washbag," adds Amy.

"I hope Dad's going to be all right," Beth says.

There's a long pause. Aunt Em's footsteps tap down the stairs.

"Meg?" she calls. "Do you have any Evian water? If not, could one of you go to the store?"

"This," I say with a sigh, "is going to be weird."

Part Three

Summer

Chapter 1

Three months have passed.

When the test results came back, it turned out that Dad had contracted encephalitis in Syria. He's still in hospital close to the airport in Germany where he collapsed – the doctors said it was important not to move him – but Mum says he seems far stronger now and is hopefully well on the way to a full recovery. She has rented a cheap apartment there, which the army are paying for.

And we're stuck with Aunt Em.

Actually, that's not fair. She's a lot easier to deal with than I'd expected, so long as you follow her rules. She leaves the house first thing, in her suit and elegant coat, and gets back in the evening, where she sits at our kitchen table drinking a glass of white wine and firing off emails while supervising one of us cooking dinner, which involves far too much steamed fish and raw vegetables for my liking.

Then she either has a conference call in the living room, or forces us all to sit through a documentary with subtitles. She's out right now, for once – and I'm taking advantage of her absence to do some writing up in my room. Amy is with her friends downstairs (including Katy Brown, with whom she is now officially BFF) and they're making their usual racket – shrieking their heads off watching some stupid movie – while Meg is playing that hideous dancey trancey music she likes in the bathroom. Beth is pottering about in the kitchen, baking for an upcoming charity bake sale.

I sigh. I'm sure Charlotte Bronte never had to cope with her sisters' noise while *she* was trying to write a story.

Or maybe she did.

I grin to myself, picturing big sister Charlotte stomping around the Bronte's vicarage telling off Anne and Emily for wrecking her focus, then turn back to my latest Tallulah story. It's about Tallulah entering a singing competition and coming second, then the winner being wrongly accused of cheating and Talluah having to clear her name. It's fun making Tallulah a great singer but even better to show her struggling to overcome her envy of the winner in order to help her.

Just as I'm writing the final scene Beth calls from downstairs.

"Mum and Dad are Skyping!" she cries.

I bang on the bathroom door to let Meg know, then hurry down. I pass Beth on her way into the living room, presumably going to fetch Amy. I dash into the kitchen and hurl myself into the prime chair right in front of the computer. Dad's thin, grey face fills the screen.

"Hey, Jo-Jo," he says with a smile. "How are you? What are you writing?"

My stomach gives a lurch. He still looks so ill. Mum has reassured us a million times that he is definitely on the mend, but it's hard to believe it when he looks so weak.

"I'm fine," I say, forcing myself to sound more cheerful than I feel. "We're all fine. How about you?"

"Great guns, definitely home soon," Dad says. "Tell me what you're writing. Is it another Tallulah? I loved the last one."

I launch into an outline of the Tallulah singing plot. It's such a treat having Dad to myself for a few moments. He nods encouragingly when I've finished.

"Let me know when you post – email the link, yeah?"

"Sure."

At that moment the others fly in and swarm around me, pushing for space so they can see Dad on the screen – and so he can see them. The five of us chatter away, Amy showing Dad the self-portrait she's been drawing – which I have to admit isn't bad – and Meg recounting how she took the little Gardiner boys swimming yesterday and one of them managed a whole width. Dad manages to answer them both with genuine interest and pride, but still make sure Beth gets a chance to shine too, asking to hear her play the piano, which she does, even though all Amy's friends are still in the living room.

After about ten minutes, Mum comes on screen saying that Dad needs to rest. We tell them both that we love them, and the screen goes blank.

There's a silence, and then, rather quietly, we wander away back to our separate activities. I try to get back to my story but it's hard settle after the call. I sit at my desk with a sigh and force myself to finish the Tallulah story, then post it on my blog. I send Dad the link, as promised, and sit back in my chair. Truth is that I'm bored with the summer holidays already (not that I'd admit it to anyone) even though we've only been off school for a week. I wouldn't mind if I had the house to myself but everyone's always here, on top of each other. I gaze at the pictures above my bed. I've added a few more now: the Sydney Opera House and Ayers Rock, both in Australia, plus a photo of a beautiful cathedral in Rome and a landscape of rolling hills just outside Florence, in Italy.

At least I'm getting away this weekend. Not abroad, admittedly, but I'm still looking forward to it. This weekend is the Manning Plains festival, the tickets for which caused all that upset with Lateef a few months ago, though our argument is long behind us now, of course.

There's loads from our year going, with Sallie Gardiner at the centre of things, thanks to her Dad being the one offering the cut-price tickets. Mr and Mrs Gardiner are coming too – so Meg will be looking after the twins all weekend while they're gone. I wish it was just me and Lateef, to be honest.

Thankfully I haven't had to buy a tent. I'll be staying in one of the four-person shelters Sallie and her friends are providing. I can't imagine the immaculate Mrs Gardiner camping, but Sallie says she loves going to festivals.

Maybe the weekend will be a chance for me to make friends with more of the girls in my year. I haven't seen any of them since the end of term – I'm not exactly BFFs with Sallie and her group. But the festival will be a great opportunity for us to bond and have fun: there'll be several of my favourite indie bands and fashion stalls and circus acts and all sorts of cool stuff. I can't wait!

My head's too full of the upcoming festival – and worry about Dad – for me to write, so I sit on my bed, rereading the first book in the *Blacktower* series. I'm soon so caught up in its world that I don't hear either when Aunt Em comes home or Amy's friends leave. In fact, I'm not aware of anything or anybody for the next hour or so. Not until Aunt Em's sharp tones cut through my reading.

"Jo! Come and help Beth with dinner!"

I trudge downstairs to find Beth alone in the kitchen. I lay out knives and forks. Eating together at seven p.m. sharp on the evenings she's in is one of the few rules Aunt Em has imposed, the other being a curfew of ten p.m. "because I don't want to be worrying about where you are all the time".

Soon the five of us are tucking into the one-pot chicken stew that Beth has made. As usual with Beth's cooking, it's delicious. Even Aunt Em says so.

"It's excellent news that your father is on the mend," she says, smiling. "Though I do blame him for taking such a foolish assignment. It's not surprising he fell ill."

Anger stirs inside me. How dare she criticize him? I shoot her a filthy look.

Aunt Em doesn't seem to notice. "Anyway, it's good that he'll be home soon," she says. "And while I'm on the subject of good things, I thought you'd like to know that I'm planning a trip to Paris and then through France to Italy for three weeks in August."

A twinge of envy twists in my gut.

"Paris," Meg gushes. "The fashion capital of the world."

I raise a sardonic eyebrow in her direction. "And therefore full of designers," I mutter. "You'd fit right in."

"Shut up, Jo," Meg snaps. She turns to Aunt Em. "It sounds like an amazing trip."

"*Sooo* amazing," Amy adds, leaning forward with her hands clasped.

"And the good news is," Aunt Em says, "that I'll be taking one of you with me."

What? It takes a moment for this to sink in.

I stare at her. This is my dream come true. "Taking one of us?" I echo.

"To Paris and Italy?" Meg adds.

"For three whole weeks?" Amy's voice is a gasp.

"Was I speaking some incomprehensible dialect just now? Because you all seem to be repeating everything I just said." Aunt Em says irritably. "Yes, three weeks. And yes, one of you will come with me. I'll need an assistant while I'm out there and it seems like a good opportunity for one of you girls." She takes another sip from her glass. "I'll have a think about who would be most suitable."

I struggle to contain my excitement. She's going to pick me. Of course she is. I've always been the one to run errands for her. And I'm strong too – easily able to lug around the piles of designer suitcases Aunt Em is bound to take with her. Paris and Italy – two places I have always dreamed of visiting. Finally I will be escaping Ringstone and seeing the world.

What with Dad coming home and the promise of a trip on the horizon, this summer will be the best yet.

Chapter 2

Of course I leave packing for Manning Plains festival to the last minute, so I'm running around my bedroom like a mad thing with Beth trying to help me get ready. Sallie and her friends are supplying not only the tents, but inflatable mattresses and sleeping bags for everyone – so all I have to bring are clothes for two days and a contribution to the food. Beth takes her duties as my chief packing adviser very seriously and is still debating over sweaters as the Gardiners' minivan – hired for the occasion – pulls up outside and honks loudly.

"Time's up," I say, grabbing my favourite red jumper from Beth's discarded pile and shoving it into my bag.

"Oh, Jo!" Beth looks horrified. "That one's full of moth holes."

I make a face, give her a hug, then race downstairs. A whirlwind of goodbyes from Meg, Aunt Em and Amy, who – as usual – is hanging out in the living room with Katy, then I grab my bag and stride out.

Lateef – who has obviously heard the minibus from his own house – is hurrying across the road. I wave at Sallie, then find an empty seat near the front while Lateef wanders around the bus, hugging everyone and radiating a puppyish excitement that makes everyone smile, even Sallie's closest and meanest friend, who I don't like at all: Zoe Carpenter.

I can't help but feel gratified when, after Mr Gardiner tells everyone to take their seats, Lateef slips in beside me. He might be friends with everyone, but I'm still his bestie. We plan to spend the journey listening to the music we're going to hear this weekend. He watches as I fumble with my snarled old headphones that came free with someone's phone.

"Here, take these." He presses his expensive Beats headphones into my hands.

I stare at him, startled. "I can't."

"It's just for the weekend," he says. "I want you

word perfect by the time we're at the front of the crowd."

"Thanks," I say, grinning with delight. "You're the best."

Manning Plains festival is *amazing*. The sun is shining as we drive up a mud track and park alongside the first of two big fields dotted with brightly coloured canvas. Sallie's mum organizes us into four groups and then she and Sallie's dad help us to set up our tents alongside the rows and rows of others. It takes a while, thanks to the strong winds blustering through the nearby trees. Thankfully I'm in a different tent from Zoe, who is sharing with Sallie and two of her more giggly friends. The girls I'm with are cool, though I'm not close to any of them: three friends who have known each other since primary school.

As soon as the tents are up Sallie's parents make us put on jumpers or jackets – "It might be sunny but there's a cold breeze," – and then wave us off to explore the festival with the usual warnings about avoiding strangers, drugs and alcohol ringing in our ears. Past the two fields of tents and we're in another open space with a raised platform at one end. A band is on stage, testing their instruments. As we get nearer they break into a song. None of us know either the musicians or the music, but it doesn't matter: the effect of the guitars – their sound growing first louder, then softer as the wind whips the tune away from us – is exhilarating. Stretching beyond the stage on either side are clusters of food and clothes stalls. Sallie turns to everyone, eyes wide with excitement.

"Let's check out the fashion stands," she urges.

Zoe and several of the other girls squeal with delight. I can't imagine why anyone would want to look at boring clothes when there is all this amazing music and atmosphere to soak up.

"I think I'll stay here," I say, glancing across at Lateef. "Check out the music."

"Yeah, me too," he says.

"OK." Sallie gives us a curious look. "See you later."

I'm entranced by the music that's now playing and Lateef and I spend the next couple of hours watching four more bands perform. I spot the other girls on the far side of the field at one point and wave. My tent-mates wave back cheerfully, but Sallie and Zoe don't seem to see me.

And that's pretty much how it goes for the rest of the day. Sallie and Zoe and their group spend most of the time hanging around the fashion stalls, while the rest of us take in as much music as we can. Lateef, Tiny and I – along with a few others – wander between the main stage and the smaller undercover areas where lesser-known musicians are performing. There's a big range of styles on offer: from a DJ playing hits from the nineties to a live indie band made up of five girls in animal outfits whose guitar playing and vocal harmonies soar over the field.

I don't speak much to Sallie or Zoe but later, once we're snuggled up in our tent, I have a laugh with the three girls I'm sharing with. We stay awake for ages chatting about stupid stuff and giggling over nothing. It's not that different from hanging out with my sisters really, and certainly nice to feel I'm making new friends.

The next day passes much the same as the previous afternoon. Everyone's up early and Sallie's dad makes us all tea and sausages on his little fire – though Sallie and Zoe go to one of the catering vans for hot chocolate and croissants instead. Afterwards, Lateef and I spend the day soaking up all the music on offer. We hardly see Sallie or her friends.

The next morning we sleep a bit later, enjoy another breakfast of tea and sausages, then pack up the tents. Lateef and I go for a last stroll before we leave. The music is all over and all the stuff on the stage is being removed, big burly guys with huge beards manhandling amps and drum kits into boxes. The stalls beyond are being dismantled too. I feel sad it's over, but so happy I had the experience. My little world is going to get bigger, I can feel it – starting with this festival but then also Paris and Rome coming up soon, hopefully, with Aunt Em. . .

Lateef goes off to talk to one of the boys from our class. I say I'll meet him at the minivan – we'll be leaving in about twenty minutes. As I walk back past one of the fashion stalls, I catch Sallie's penetrating voice.

"She's just embarrassing," she is saying. "I mean the stuff she wears. . ."

"Oh my God. Did you see that red jumper of hers?" Zoe is saying. "*Full* of holes."

I freeze. Are they talking about me?

"How could you miss it?" Sallie replies with a snort. "I know they're broke, but Meg manages to look normal. It's just attention-seeking. I mean, *really*. It was more holes than actual jumper. And don't get me started on that stain."

Zoe and the other girls laugh. The wind whips around the side of the stall, making me shiver. I glance down at my jumper. Beth tried to stop me bringing it, I remember. OK, so it's fraying at the cuffs and there are a couple of grubby-edged holes and a yellowed bleach stain across the chest . . . but surely it's not *that* bad?

"She's only here because Lateef bought her ticket," Sallie says.

My heart beats hard, drumming in my ears. One of the other girls says something in a low voice I can't catch.

"You're so right," Sallie says. "I like Lateef too. It's not fair what Jo's doing."

"Yeah," Zoe says. "She's totally got her claws into him. Poor Lateef doesn't stand a chance. Everyone knows she's a total freeloader. She's using him."

The words hit me like a punch to the gut.

"Do you really think Jo is friends with Lateef just because he's rich?" another voice asks.

"Totally," Zoe says. "Did you see those Beats headphones? They're his – I've seen him with them at school. I reckon he's so nice he can't say 'no' to her."

I gasp, an involuntary suck of breath. It's so horrible, what they're saying – that I'm only friends with Lateef because of his money. I clutch the side of the stall. For a second I'm determined to walk round to the front and reveal myself, to tell them they're wrong and demand an apology, especially from mean, horrible Zoe Carpenter. And then I stop, imagining all their faces and how embarrassing a confrontation would be.

I stumble away instead, my cheeks burning with rage and humiliation. I can't wait to get home, away from these awful people so ready to think the worst of me.

And then a fresh and even more horrific thought strikes me.

Is it possible that, in spite of everything, Lateef thinks the same thing?

Chapter 3

I hardly speak on the way home from the festival. I spend the journey huddled against the window on the back seat of the minivan, pretending I have a stomach ache. Eventually Lateef stops asking me if I'm OK, and chats to the others. We both get out on Fishtail Lane and I scuttle away after the briefest of goodbyes. I can hardly meet his eyes.

As soon as I get inside I grab Meg and drag her into our bedroom. I tell her what Zoe and Sallie said, my eyes filling with hot, bitter tears as I speak.

Meg's jaw drops. "How *dare* they," she says, her cheeks flooding with colour. "I've a good mind to tell Sallie what I think of her next time I go over to look after the twins."

"But what if Lateef thinks it too? That I'm just friends with him because he's rich?" I shiver at the thought. "I need to make sure he knows that it isn't true."

Meg considers this for a moment, then shakes her head. "There's no way," she says. "I can guarantee he doesn't think that about you."

"How do you know?" I demand.

"Because . . . because that's just not who Lateef is," Meg says. "And that's not who you are, and he knows that." She pats my arm in the same kind, brisk way Mum does. "Now, come downstairs and have some tea. Beth's spent all morning making cupcakes."

I purse my lips. Maybe she's right about Lateef but I need to be sure. The awful things the girls said are burned into my brain, and I couldn't bear it if Lateef felt the same, even for a minute. I need to speak to him and find out.

Lateef answers the door when I ring on the bell. He eyes me with concern. "Are you feeling better? I was going to come over later and check on you."

"I'm fine," I say. "I just wanted to see you."

"We spent the whole weekend together," he says with a chuckle. "Not that I'm complaining. What d'you want to do? Movie? Music? Park?"

His eyes sparkle as he waits for my answer. Surely he wouldn't look at me like that if thought I was just interested in his money?

I wrinkle my nose. "Let's just hang out, see what happens. It's nice just being the two of us instead of a big crowd."

"'Course it is," Lateef says. "That's because I'm the best."

"Bighead," I grin, following him through the hall and up the stairs.

We go into Lateef's bedroom and flop down on the sofa. Lateef idly picks up one of the Xbox controllers on the table in front of him and sets up a game. I don't even notice which one. I try to join in, but my heart isn't in it.

Now I'm here it's not so easy to bring up the subject of money.

After a few minutes Lateef sets down his controller and turns to me. "Are you sure you're OK? You seem . . . I dunno, really down. Are you still feeling ill?" He looks at me uneasily. "You're not going to be sick are you?"

I shake my head.

"Well, then – did something happen at the festival? At the end?" He moves a little closer. "Did one of the girls say something?"

I stare into his eyes, so full of affection and concern. Trust my best friend to have sensed what's really troubling me.

I shrug. "Yeah, there was the odd bitchy comment. . ." I affect a yawn. "You know what happens when people are in groups."

Lateef narrows his eyes. "It was Zoe Carpenter, wasn't it? She said something nasty?"

I look away, my face flushing. "What makes you think that?"

"Dunno," he says thoughtfully. "I think she likes stirring things up, getting attention by saying outrageous things."

"She certainly does," I mutter.

"Well?" Lateef persists. "What did she say?"

"It doesn't matter." And suddenly I realize that's the truth. It's not just that it feels really awkward to bring up the subject of money; there's no point in going into all the details. Meg was right about that. It will only upset him. Maybe even plant the seed of a worry that I *am* only friends with him in order to get access to all the nice stuff he has. I need to forget all about Zoe and Sallie and their stupid opinions.

"Are you sure?" Lateef asks. "Because you're my . . . my friend, and if you're upset then I want to know . . .

to help. . ." He trails off, his expression suddenly serious.

I stare at him, a lump in my throat. We're sitting so close to each other that I can see the flecks of gold in his dark eyes.

"It was just a stupid thing," I stammer.

Lateef nods. "Go on. . ."

"Just. . ." I reach out impulsively and take his hand. "You know that I like you for *you*, don't you?" I gesture around his room. "It's cool that you have nice stuff, but it's you I like."

Lateef gazes at me, an expression I can't read on his face. Normally I know exactly what he's thinking. He leans closer to me, like he's about to whisper in my ear.

"Jo! Jo!" It's Amy's voice, followed by the sound of footsteps running up the stairs. She bursts into the bedroom and Lateef and I spring apart. She's waving my phone – which I left charging in my room – and grinning from ear to ear. Beth is close behind her, flushed and excited.

"Your Tallulah story's gone viral!" Amy gasps. "The one about the parrot and the funfair. It's got, like, hundreds of hits just in the past two days."

I turn to Beth, who is nodding, her eyes shining.

"It's true. Your phone rang just now. Amy answered and—"

"And it was a *publisher*!" Amy finishes, grabbing my arm. "Someone called Marianne Steiner. She said she's an editor at a big London publishing house for children's books and she wants to talk to you about your story!"

My jaw drops.

"That's amazing!" Lateef is on his feet beside us. He pulls me towards him in a bear hug. "I knew your greatness would be recognized, Jo March."

Amy thrusts the phone at me. "You have to call her back. Now!"

Chapter 4

I shut myself in my room to make the call.

"Marianne Steiner." There's a crisp, upper-class edge to her voice.

"Hi," I say. "This is Jo March. I, er, I think you called me earlier?"

"Ah, Jo, thanks for calling back," she says, her voice immediately warm and assured. "I got your details from your blog – I hope you don't mind me calling?"

"No," I say. "No, I don't mind at all. But I don't really understand why you—"

"Let me explain." Marianne clears her throat. "I've been setting up a new website aimed at young teenagers in the UK called Teen Spiral. Have you heard of it?"

"Er, no," I confess.

"Not surprising," Marianne says briskly. "We only went live a few months ago but the site is getting lots of attention and great feedback. We're adding new segments all the time."

"I see," I say, though to be honest I'm still completely confused. What does any of this have to do with my Tallulah stories?

"We're looking to introduce a new strand to our fiction section called, 'Our Stories, Ourselves'," Marianne goes on. "That is, short stories written *by* teenagers *for* teenagers. I've had a look at one of your blog posts and asked a number of people, including our teenage focus groups, to read the story. Everyone was very impressed by your writing."

"Really?" My pulse quickens. That explains all the recent hits.

"Yes." Marianne sounds like she's smiling. "We'd like to invite you to submit a story."

"One of my Tallulah stories?" My head feels like it might burst with excitement.

"No, not exactly." Marianne clears her throat again. "As I say, everyone on the Spiral team was very impressed by your writing, but we're looking for fiction that's a little more realistic. More true to life."

"You mean, like, Tallulah but without special powers?" I ask.

"It's not that so much." Marianne hesitates. "More just that if you're writing about the experiences of a contemporary girl, it would be good to make those experiences feel *real*, like they could happen to you, to our readers. . ."

"Oh," I say. "I see."

I think for a moment. I love Tallulah, and I feel a bit nervous about writing what Marianne suggests – something true to life. My stories have always been full of imaginary heroes and villains. On the other hand this Teen Spiral website sounds like it will reach far more people than my blog ever could. And who knows who might read what I write there? Maybe this is the first step to getting properly published one day.

"OK." My mouth feels dry. "That sounds great. When do you want a new story?"

"Three or four months," Marianne says promptly. "Because the other thing is . . . once we've got a few more segments in place, we're planning a big launch for the whole site at the start of next year, with the new 'Our Stories, Ourselves' segment firmly front and centre. If what you write meets the brief, you'll be the site's first published teenage author, with your story right up there alongside the more experienced writers." When I gasp, she says hastily, "I'm afraid there's only a small payment for this, but as I say, it will give you access to lots of teen users and you can link back to your blog from the site, and, well, if Teen Spiral takes off like I hope, then it could be the start of exciting things for you. I think you have real talent, Jo, and I'd love to have you on board. If you're game, that is?"

I feel an enormous grin stretching my face. "Thank you. And yes, er, I'm game."

"Great, well I'll send you an email with all of this. Now, is there an adult I could speak to, please?"

"Sure. Mum and Dad are away. I'll pass you over to my aunt." I go out of the room and hand my phone to Aunt Em. She's waiting on the landing with Lateef and my sisters. They are wide-eyed, eager to hear all the details. I can't face them just yet. I'm too overwhelmed. I make a quick excuse and hurry into the bathroom. I shut the door and sit on the side of the bath.

I can't believe it. This is *it*. I know it. My big break. After all my years of scribbling stories, I'm finally going to have something properly recognized. Out there in the world.

I just need to write it.

*

The next morning I sit down to work, determined to come up with a really good, dramatic idea for a new story that will also be, as Marianne Steiner put it, a bit more "true to life".

An hour later I'm still staring at my laptop, totally failing to come up with anything Marianne might consider properly realistic. Real life means no treacherous villains or castles shrouded in mist or teenage girl detectives on super-cool adventures. In fact, I decide, real life makes boring fiction.

"Jo! I need you – come here, please!" For once Aunt Em's crisp command doesn't fill me with resentment. And it's not just because I want to demonstrate I'm keen to help her lug her bags about on holiday.

For the first time I can remember, I'm actually eager to get away from my writing. I find her in Mum's room, consulting a typed list while Amy puts things in a suitcase.

"And I'll take two blouses, no, not the khaki, the grey. Ah, Jo." Aunt Em gestures towards a thickly stuffed package on top of the chest of drawers. "Those papers need couriering. All the information is on the top – the post office can do the rest. Thank you."

She turns back to the wardrobe.

"OK, no problem," I say cheerfully, without any of my usual eye-rolling. I'm determined to show her how useful and eager to help I am, so I just skip off downstairs and along the few streets to central Ringstone. I take extra care at the post office to send the parcel according to the exact instructions. The last time I sent a package I lost the proof of postage, which led to Aunt Em ranting about my carelessness for twenty minutes straight.

By the time I get home, Aunt Em and Amy are out and Beth and Meg are watching TV. I head to my room and flop on the bed, determined to think of a story idea. I sit with my laptop perched on my knees, feeling increasingly fidgety for ten minutes or so, but an idea still doesn't come. I decide to go over the road and see if Lateef is in.

I tug on one of my sandals, then look around for the other. It's on its side at the end of Meg's bed. As I bend down to fetch it I spot the edges of a thick, well-thumbed book under the mattress. I pull it out, curious. Meg hardly ever reads anything.

Careers in Child Care

I stare at the title of the book. What is Meg doing with this? She's only just finished her first year of A-levels. She's doing really well, too, particularly on her art and psychology courses. Surely she should be starting to think about applying for university or art school? She likes looking after the Gardiner boys, but that's just for some extra cash over the summer. She surely can't want to do babysitting as a career?

The door opens and I turn, the book still in my hand.

"What are you doing with that?" Meg appears in the doorway, her forehead creased with a frown. "Have you been going through my stuff?"

"Where did you get this?" I demand, flourishing the book. "And why are you interested in looking after kids as an actual job?"

"Mum got it for me," Meg says, her face flooding with colour. "She borrowed it from—"

"So *Mum's* in on this?"

"Why do you have to make it sound like a conspiracy?" Meg says snippily. "Anyway, why *shouldn't* I be interested?"

"Because . . . because . . . you're so good at design and styling, and you're so interested in fashion. Why don't you want to do that? Go to art school or something?"

"For goodness' sake, Jo, stop being such a snob," Meg snaps. "I've told you a million times – I don't *want* to be a designer. I can't think of anything worse."

"Yes, you do," I argue. "It's what you've always wanted, deep down, like I want to be a writer."

"No," Meg says, taking a deep breath and running her fingers through her hair. "No, that's just what you *want* to think. I love fashion, yes. I love putting together an outfit. It's fun. But I don't want to *make* it. I want to *buy* it. And *wear* it. I do like children. I find them interesting. I find child development interesting. And as a nanny, for instance, I could make good money."

"*Money*?" I say, the disgust bursting out of me. "What about *art*?"

Meg shakes her head, clearly frustrated. "You're such an idiot, Jo; you think everyone's the same as you. But they're not."

"OK, fine." I look down at the brochure. "Fine if you don't want to be a fashion designer. But – being a nanny! That's not creative at all. You need to—"

"Stop it!" Meg shouts. "Just stop it. Stop thinking you know best for me. This is just like when you applied for that internship. I don't *want* to be a designer. Can't you get that through your stupid head? I want to work with children." Her eyes flare with impatience and she speaks very slowly and emphatically. "Do you hear me, Jo? *Children.* The most important things on the planet. And being a nanny *is* interesting and you *can* be creative. Just not in the way you think."

I drop my gaze. "I still think it's stupid," I mutter. "You could do so much more."

"There is nothing more important than working with children. Nothing."

I roll my eyes.

Meg's jaw tightens. "It's certainly a lot more important than writing stupid stories."

I gasp, as if she just slapped me. There's a long pause.

"Anyway," she says coldly, "it's *my* choice." And, with that, she turns on her heel and storms out.

I lie back on my bed, my insides churning. All our lives, Meg and I have shared everything. We've never been that alike, but being so close in age we've spent a lot of time together. And we've always got on and always understood each other's hopes and dreams. At least I thought we did. But now, for the first time, I realize that maybe I don't understand Meg at all.

My phone rings. It's Lateef. I curl up on my bed, holding the mobile to my ear.

"Hey, Jo March." His cheerful voice makes me feel better right away. "You wanna come over?"

"I was about to do just that actually." I hesitate. "Hey, you'll never guess what Meg's been up to."

"What?" Lateef asks.

I picture his eyes widening with shock as I reveal Meg's stupid plans to him. He'll agree with me – that a career looking after kids is a waste of her talent and we have to persuade her to change her mind. "I'll tell you when I get there."

At least I have him. At least I can rely on Lateef.

Chapter 5

By the time I get to Lateef's, the brilliant sunshine of earlier has faded and clouds have gathered, threatening rain. Nevertheless, we're lying on the grass in his back garden – an expanse of bright lawn surrounded by carefully tended bushes and flower beds. Uncle Jim potters here most weekends and they have a gardener on Mondays. Compared to our garden – which despite Beth's work is overrun with plants and has weeds poking through the cracks in the tiny patio – it's a paradise.

I tell Lateef all about discovering Meg's ambition to be a nanny. Lateef doesn't say much as I talk.

"She's so talented," I groan, lying back on the rug we're sharing. "She's got such a great eye for putting outfits together, she'd be a brilliant designer. She just. . ." I stop, wondering once again what exactly it is that puts Meg off going down the path I had always assumed she would take. "I used to think it was that she didn't believe in herself but maybe she just doesn't like the sound of all the hard work involved. . ." I trail off.

Lateef props himself on his elbow and looks at me, lying beside him. "Looking after kids *is* hard work," he says gently.

"Mmm," I say, not really listening. "Maybe she just doesn't have any confidence." I look up at Lateef, wondering suddenly what his ambitions are. "What about you?" I ask. "I have my writing. Is there anything you really want?" I ask.

Lateef looks down at me, an odd expression on his face.

"Are you OK?" I ask.

There's a moment's pause where Lateef looks like he's hesitating, on the verge of saying something important. Then he lets out his breath in a big sigh and drops down, on to his back.

"Lateef?" I sit up. "What is it?"

"Nothing. I was thinking we should go on a picnic tomorrow," he says after another second or two. "Get the bus to the beach. You, me, your sisters, Tiny, maybe a few others. What do you think? Plan?"

I grin, lying back down again. "Plan."

Picnic day turns out to be the hottest of the summer so far. The clouds have cleared and the sun is a fierce orange disk in a bright blue sky. We're not the only ones who've decided to get the bus down to the beach and, after a sweaty, cramped journey, we race across the dunes to a local area known as the Rocks like animals who've just been let out of a cage.

Lateef is in his element, chattering away with everyone, a rucksack of lemonades on his back. Meg has a bag crammed with the crisps and pies that Aunt Em gave us money for. She looks particularly pretty today, her skin glowing and her sunglasses perched jauntily on her blonde waves.

Not that I have any intention of telling her so. Since yesterday's row we've barely spoken – and then only over practical stuff like what to bring on the picnic. I guess Meg is still angry that I think she's wasting her artistic talents. Which I do. It's not that there's anything wrong with looking after kids, but surely if you're as style savvy as Meg you should make the most of that gift?

I guess we're just going to have to agree to disagree.

We fall into our natural pairings as we wander around the Rocks, looking for the best place to set up our picnic. Meg chatters away with Amy, whose face is half-covered by a huge floppy hat. I can hear Amy moaning about how her bag is weighed down with the big bottle of sun lotion which Aunt Em insisted we bring. Beth pads along, silently, beside me. She's carrying the picnic rug, while I've got our towels and my book. Not that I think there'll be much time for reading. Lateef, Tiny and four or five others, including Tiny's cousins Aidan and Frankie, don't look like they plan on sitting around for long. As well as their own food and drink they have two footballs and a selection of Frisbees. Nobody – other than me – seems keen to swim. I can't wait. I love the sea, the exhilaration of being in the open water and the feel of the waves on my face. Plus, inspiration might strike while I'm in the water; maybe, finally, I'll get an idea for my story.

We soon find the perfect place to make camp: a small stretch of sand with two cliffs on either side, one of which slopes down to the beach in a series of stones, making the whole cliff look like a face with one half collapsed. There are two other groups here – a small knot of twenty-somethings and a larger group of mums and kids – but it's much less crowded than the properly public areas.

Beth and I lay out the picnic rug in the shade of an overhanging rock face. The beach here is pebble-strewn sand, with a large outcrop of grey rock, for which Beth instantly makes a beeline. I follow her and slip out of my shorts and T-shirt – I'm already wearing my swimsuit underneath. I wind my long hair into a knot and tie it back off my face with a band, then I inch myself into the water. I yelp as I wade in. It's cold, despite the hot sun, and I don't stay in long. Just a couple of lengths up and down the rocks, feeling the saltwater splash against my face (nice) and something slimy slither against my bare legs (not so nice). Beth watches me from her perch on the rocks.

"Don't fancy it, Bethy?" I ask as I emerge, shivering.

She hands me a towel and shakes her head. "No thanks. Actually I've got a bit of a sore throat," she says.

"Oh no." I stare at her, concerned. Unlike Amy who lets us all know, loudly, whenever she's not well, Beth never complains about anything. She does look pale, actually. "Can I get you anything?"

“No thanks.” She lies back on the rock, her face tipped to the sun. “I’m just going to sit here quietly for a bit.”

I lie beside her, letting the heat dry my skin, my lips tasting the salt from the seawater. After fifteen minutes or so it’s too hot to be in direct sunlight and we shift across to a shady patch of rock. I put my T-shirt on then and glance over at the beach. Lateef, Meg, Tiny and Aidan are playing football with two girls from school and two boys I don’t know. The remaining girl – Aidan’s sister Frankie – is huddled against the rocks on our rug. Next to her Amy is lying stretched out, her big hat covering her face.

A cheer goes up from some of the footballers. Lateef looks up and waves me over.

“Come on, Jo!” he calls. “Beth!”

I turn to Beth. “How are you feeling?” I ask.

“Better,” she says. “But I think I’ll sit here a bit longer. You go and join the others.”

I look at her carefully. I’m not sure I believe she really does feel better. Her cheeks are still very pale considering how hot it is.

“OK,” I say, tugging on my shorts. “But come and get me if you feel worse. We can go straight home whenever you like.”

"Thanks, Jo." Beth smiles at me, then leans against her rock again and closes her eyes.

I grab my towel and make my way back to the beach. My trainers catch on a sharp bit of rock as I pass, nearly tripping me and ripping the front binding from the shoe. I swear under my breath as I flap the rest of the way.

By the time I've made my way back to the others, the football game is over and the rug is pretty crowded. As I arrive a small group heads off for ice cream, leaving behind just my sisters, Lateef, Tiny and his cousins. The boy cousin, Aidan, is sitting very close to Meg, I notice. He's as tall as Tiny but ten times better looking with dark curly hair and a very cheeky grin. The two of them are whispering and giggling like they're the only ones on the beach.

"Did you go swimming in the sea?" Frankie asks as I flop down on the edge of the rug. She sounds shocked, her brown eyes wide like chocolate buttons.

"'Course she did," Lateef says, a note of pride in his voice. "Jo March likes an adventure."

I roll my eyes at him, tugging the band from my hair so it falls, damp and salty, down my back. Lateef watches me, his eyes lingering on my hair as I shake it free.

"What are you guys doing?" I ask.

"We were just about to play 'Truth'," Frankie says. "You know it? Whoever's name gets drawn out of a hat has to answer one question from each of the others as truthfully as they can."

"Oh yeah, we play that at home," I say. "Let's use Amy's hat."

"Count me out," Aidan says with a grimace. "Sounds dangerous." He glances sideways at Meg. "Fancy a walk, Meg?"

"OK." Meg leaps up.

"Why *my* hat?" Amy grumbles.

"It means you're in charge of the game, Amy," Lateef says.

Amy looks slightly mollified. Meg and Aidan saunter away along the beach, Aidan laughing – too loudly – at something Meg has said. I notice Lateef looking after them with an amused expression. He catches my eye and winks.

"Everyone ready?" Tiny asks.

"Sure," Lateef says, rubbing his hands with relish.

"I guess," Frankie agrees. "Though we don't have a pen and paper to write down our names."

"Give me your phones, then," Amy says, holding out her hat.

"You have to cover your eyes when you pick them out," I warn. "No peeking."

"Whatever," Amy says.

Lateef, Tiny, Frankie and I each put our mobile phone inside Amy's huge hat. We form a loose circle. I sit between Lateef and Tiny with Frankie on Tiny's other side and Amy next to Lateef.

"Let's go," Lateef urges.

Amy ostentatiously covers her eyes with her hand and fishes in the hat. I'm almost certain she's sneaking a look. She draws out Lateef's shiny black iPhone.

"Jeez," Lateef groans, though he doesn't really look as though he minds.

"Me first," I say. "Who do you admire most in the world?"

"Uncle Jim," Lateef says straightaway. "He's been through so much and even though he doesn't always show it, he's kind. And my dad and . . . and my whole family from home."

"Who do you think is the prettiest person on this picnic?" Tiny asks with a low chuckle.

"Meg," Lateef says decisively.

I follow his gaze across the beach. Meg and Aidan are just visible in the distance. He's right – with her big, blue eyes, long lashes and golden waves, Meg is easily the prettiest girl here.

"OK, but who do you *like* best?" Frankie asks with a sly grin.

"Jo, of course." Lateef's cheeks colour slightly as Tiny pokes him in the chest. "Pick again, Amy."

Amy rummages among the three remaining phones. She draws out mine.

"Ha!" she says. "Jo!"

I glance around the group. Lateef, Tiny and Frankie are all smiling, clearly enjoying themselves. I suddenly feel nervous about what they might ask me.

"What is your greatest fault?" Tiny leaps in.

"That's easy," I say, relieved at the question. "I'm too impatient, too impulsive. I say things too fast and I'm clumsy."

"True," Lateef says with feeling. "I'll go." He hesitates, his face flushing slightly again. "What do you want most in the world?"

I stare at him. His eyes are dancing, but there's a seriousness in them too, like he really wants to know the answer.

Surely he already knows what I want? I've talked often enough about my dream of being published and how I'm hoping writing my new, serious story for Teen Spiral will help me on my way. I glance at Frankie. For some reason, I don't want to share my dearest ambitions with her.

"Come on, Jo," Amy says impatiently.

"Well, obviously I want to travel, go on adventures abroad. . ." I stare down at the ripped sole of my trainers, then dig my heels into the rug. "But mostly I'd like a new pair of canvas flats."

Tiny and Frankie groan.

"That's not a true answer," Lateef says earnestly. "You have to say what you really do want most."

I look up at him, irritated that he's pushing me to answer when he must *know* I'd rather not reveal my innermost dreams. "Why? There's nothing *you* can do about it," I snap. I guess I sound harsher than I mean to because a look of disappointment crosses Lateef's face. I flush with shame, annoyed with myself for upsetting him. Tiny roars with laughter.

Frankie raises her eyebrows, gazing from me to Lateef. "OK, what things do you most admire in a man?" she asks.

"Courage," I say. "And honesty."

Frankie has her turn next, but her answers are boring and by the time Tiny has had a go too the fun feels like it's gone out of the game. Lateef, Frankie and Tiny take a Frisbee on to the beach while Amy stretches out on the rug and places her hat over her face again.

I go and check on Beth. She's still not feeling great, so I offer to go home with her.

"Don't you want to stay longer?" she asks.

I glance across the beach to where Lateef is leaping to catch the Frisbee. He hasn't looked at me since I snapped at him. In the distance, Meg and Aidan are tiny figures on the sand. I can't be sure from here, but I think Aidan has his arm around her.

"I'm ready to go," I say. I feel cold, suddenly, despite the sun. "Whenever you are."

"OK," Beth says, standing up. "Let's go home."

Chapter 6

As soon as we're home Beth goes to her room to lie down and I sit in front of my laptop and try to work properly on a story for Teen Spiral. What I want to write is a version of the shipwreck story I started imagining after the book signing back in January: it opens with Tallulah walking on the beach and finding a shipwrecked sailor who has lost his memory. He turns out to be a dangerous smuggler.

I love this idea. However, I'm also aware it's exactly the kind of thing Marianne doesn't want.

After a couple of hours getting nowhere I check on Beth. She is fast asleep, her cheeks now flushed. I lay my hand on her forehand and it feels hot and damp. She stirs in her sleep. "Thirsty," she murmurs.

I go down into the kitchen to get her a glass of water and find Meg and Aunt Em in the middle of a row. It turns out that Meg wants to go out later with Aidan and some of his friends.

"That's out of the question, Margaret," Aunt Em says with an imperious wave of her hand.

"What?" Meg demands, her cheeks flushing. "*Why?*"

"Because I have a cocktail party and Amy and Elizabeth are too young to be left all evening on their own, especially with Elizabeth feeling unwell."

"I'll be here," I point out. "So it's no problem if Meg isn't."

"Mmm." Aunt Em presses her lips together. "Well I'm afraid that doesn't inspire me with confidence, Josephine. You're hardly the most reliable—"

"Actually, I'm going to Katy's for a sleepover," Amy announces, looking up from her drawing.

"If Amy's out and—" Meg starts.

"Elizabeth will be still be here," Aunt Em says briskly. "So I'd be happier if you stayed, Margaret."

Her mobile rings and she answers it with a curt: "Emmeline speaking."

Meg turns away. A tiny muscle throbs at her temple. I grab her arm and whisper in her ear:

"It's OK, just say you'll stay, then leave once Aunt Em has gone."

Meg's eyes sparkle. It's not like her to be rebellious, but clearly living with Aunt Em is taking its toll. She nods, as Aunt Em barks into her phone: "Well it needs to be done by Tuesday latest." She tuts as she ends the call, then looks up at Meg, her eyes full of irritation.

"Do we have an agreement, Margaret?" she asks.

"Of course, Aunt Em," Meg says, turning away so that Aunt Em can't see the smile that twitches at her lips.

"Good. Now go and see if Elizabeth is feeling better. And, Josephine, I'd like you and Amy to look for my pearl bracelet: the seed pearls with the platinum clasp. It's somewhere in that wretched broken drawer in your parents room. I couldn't see it, but maybe your young eyes will do better. Oh, and I'd be grateful if you'd fetch me my chartreuse silk shirt while you're there, please."

Amy and I troop upstairs. Amy checks for the bracelet while I search Aunt Em's wardrobe for the blouse she wants. After a couple of minutes, Amy holds up the delicate string of seed pearls with a triumphant grin.

"Good for you," I grumble. "I can't find that stupid shirt anywhere."

"For goodness' sake." Rolling her eyes, Amy goes straight to the right hand section of the wardrobe and carefully draws out a pale green blouse.

"I would have found it eventually," I say with a shrug.

"Like you know what chartreuse is," Amy says with a smug sniff.

Aunt Em checks on Beth before she leaves.

"Beth's still sleeping," she tells Meg as she puts on her coat in the hallway. "Which is probably the best thing for her. But do make sure she eats something when she wakes up – and there are painkillers in the bathroom cabinet."

"Yes, Aunt Em," Meg says obediently.

"I'll have my phone on me – call if she's at all worse, or you're worried."

"Of course, Aunt Em," Meg says. "Er, I was thinking I'd do some clearing up downstairs, then make some dinner."

She sounds suspiciously eager to please, but Aunt Em doesn't pick up on it. As soon as Aunt Em and Amy have gone out, Meg hurries back upstairs and starts rummaging in our wardrobe.

"You're meeting Aidan?" I ask with a grimace. I don't mind Meg going out at all, but I do wonder why she wants to hang out with the stupid boy from the picnic. "Are you and him, er, going out together now?"

"No way." Meg giggles. "It's just a laugh."

I shake my head. How can she imagine spending time with Aiden will be in any way fun?

Half an hour later, Meg leaves in a clatter of high heels. She's wearing tight jeans and bright red lipstick too. Mum and Dad would definitely not approve.

I eat some pasta and stare at my blank screen for a while. Then I go to check on Beth again. Surely she can't still be asleep?

She is. I make my way over to the bed where she is lying half in and half out of the covers. Outside the sun is hidden behind the trees, the heat of the day starting to ease and the birds singing like mad even through the closed window. I gaze down at Beth. Her colour is still high, a feverish sheen on her forehead. There is something odd about her breathing. It's fast and shallow and raspy.

I pull the covers over her exposed arm. Beth moans gently. I put my hand on her forehead. I gasp. She's burning up.

Something is very wrong.

"Beth?" I flood with fear. "*Beth?*"

I shake my sister's shoulders, desperate for her to open her eyes. But she just lies there, her head lolling back. I fumble for my phone. I need to ring Aunt Em.

With a jerk, Beth starts shaking. Juddering. Her whole body convulses. I stare down in panic.

"Beth!" I cry.

Fear clutches at my throat. Is she having a fit? A seizure?

For a moment the terror and the uncertainty overwhelm me. And then I grab my phone. Never mind calling Aunt Em. We're way past that.

What my sister needs is an ambulance.

I punch in the emergency numbers, so well drilled into all of us. It feels both strange and familiar to be dialing them.

999.

A voice answers. My head is racing too fast to hear properly what it says. Beth is still convulsing on the bed, though her movements are slowing, the jerks less spasmodic.

"It's my sister," I cut in over the calm tones of the operator. "My sister needs help. Please. Help. *Now.*"

Chapter 7

The paramedics arrive within minutes, although it feels like hours, and are brilliant and reassuring. Beth isn't fitting any more, thank goodness, though her body is still burning hot and her breath shallow. Most upsetting of all, she hasn't yet opened her eyes.

I watch, trembling, as the paramedics lift her on to a trolley with gentle, expert hands and carry her downstairs, asking me questions as they go.

"How old is your sister? What's her name? How long was she asleep before the fit? What symptoms did she complain of earlier? Where are your parents?"

I answer as best I can, my head spinning.

"We all checked in on her," I tell them. "None of us realized how ill she was." Guilt overwhelms me.

Beth never complains; I should have known this was serious. "Why was she shaking like that? Is she going to be OK?"

"It could just be a reaction to her high temperature," the young male paramedic says with a gap-toothed smile. "And her vitals are all fine; try not to worry."

"Yeah, we need to get some fluids into her, do a few tests, then we'll know a bit more." His older colleague pats my shoulder. "You can come with us to the hospital. We'll call your aunt on the way."

And so, for the first time in my life, I find myself sitting wedged in the corner of an ambulance as it hurtles along, while Beth lies silently beside me, hooked up to a drip like we're in a hospital drama on TV. Except this isn't a TV drama. This is real life and it's awful. I call Meg and Aunt Em, and they both say they're coming immediately.

As soon as we reach the hospital Beth is taken into a cubicle. Nurses work efficiently over her while I stand to one side.

Meg arrives first, her face drawn.

"Poor Beth," she whispers, hugging me close. "And oh, Jo, you must have been terrified. I feel so guilty that I went out. You were all on your own with her. . ."

"It wouldn't have made any difference," I reassure

her. I've already decided there's no way I'm going to tell Aunt Em that Meg wasn't at home. I'm certain she'll be so worried about Beth that she won't even think to ask.

Sure enough, when Aunt Em turns up a few minutes later, the scent of an expensive perfume in her wake, she is only focused on getting answers from the doctors.

"I need to tell her parents she's not well," she says. "And I don't want to call and say I've got no idea what's wrong with her." Her eyes narrow. "I should like some information, please."

"We're just waiting for some test results," one of nurses says. "The doctor will be in to talk to you very soon. You're her next patient."

Aunt Em nods, an anxious frown on her face. The three of us spend what feels like an eternity but is actually less than ten minutes watching over Beth. She is still pale and clammy, a fresh drip attached to her arm and her eyes shut. At last she opens her eyes.

"Where am I?" she asks, her voice thick.

"Hospital," Aunt Em says. I hardly recognize her voice, it's so gentle. "You gave us all quite a scare."

"I'm sorry," Beth says. Her face is grey with tiredness.

"Oh, hush." Aunt Em glances at me and Meg. "I should be the one apologizing. I should never have left you girls alone – you must have been terrified."

Meg and I look at each other.

At that moment the doctor appears. She examines Beth, touching her with gentle hands and asking a few questions in a low, soothing murmur.

"I'm pretty sure the fit just happened because Beth's temperature got too high," she says at last. "She's stable now, but we're going to admit her for the rest of the night for observation and to run a few more tests."

Armed with this information Aunt Em goes outside to call Mum. Meg and I sit on either side of Beth. Aunt Em comes back in.

"Good news," she says, going straight over to Beth who is blinking slowly awake. "Your mother is going to fly home."

"Really?" Beth smiles.

"Even better. . ." Aunt Em looks around at us all, a smile on her normally serious face. "Your dad has just been given the all-clear. They'll both be home the day after tomorrow. Your mother is booking flights now."

"Oh, yes!" I gasp, relief seeping through me. I

hadn't realized how much I'd missed them until this moment. Mum and Dad *home*.

"Thank goodness." Meg clasps her hands together.

Beth says nothing, just leans back on her pillows, her eyes welling with tears of joy.

"So you need to work hard on getting better, Beth," Aunt Em says, reverting to her usual, brisk manner. I notice she avoids her more normal "Elizabeth". "Then we can have you home as soon as possible."

Beth nods, her eyes still closed.

Aunt Em clears her throat. "I think you girls should head off now. Beth's going to be admitted to a ward and I'll stay with her. You can come back in the morning, when she's had some rest."

I gaze down at Beth, reluctant to leave her. Meg touches my arm.

"I'll be OK, Jo," Beth whispers, her eyes flickering briefly open.

Aunt Em walks us to the exit. She calls a taxi and, while we wait, reels off instructions about cleaning and tidying the house. As she puts us into the cab, though, she squeezes my arm.

"Thank you for looking after her, Jo," she says in a low voice. "You girls did well this evening."

There is warmth in her eyes and I feel closer to her

than I ever have.

"With Mum and Dad home in a few days I guess you'll be able to finally book your holiday," I say, genuinely pleased for her. This isn't a hint about Aunt Em taking me with her. With Beth so ill the thought doesn't even occur to me.

"Not till Beth is properly better," Aunt Em says, glancing back at the hospital.

"Of course," I say. "But that's going to be soon. I just know it is."

She smiles again. "Of course it is, Jo," she says.

I wake early and set to cleaning Beth and Amy's room. I attack every corner with a duster, shoving Amy's piles of clothes and toiletries under her bed and into her drawers. Hesitant to vacuum while Meg is asleep, I go outside and pick a handful of tiny daisies from the garden. I put them in a glass on Beth's bedside table.

Meg is up by the time Aunt Em calls from the hospital with an update.

"The doctor says that Beth is stable and they're putting yesterday's high temperature down to a mystery virus," she says with an unimpressed sniff. "I have to say she does seem absolutely fine now, so they're letting her out this afternoon."

I offer to change places with her at the hospital, so she can come home and get some sleep. Meg suggests that she should pop over to Katy Brown's house and fetch Amy, with strict instructions she's not to have her friends round for a few days while Beth recuperates and Mum and Dad settle in back at home.

Aunt Em agrees to both ideas gratefully.

I spend the next few hours sitting next to Beth in her hospital bed. I've brought my laptop and, while Beth dozes, I have another attempt at a story for Teen Spiral.

I try to imagine a Tallulah story but without Tallulah being free to go anywhere and do anything. Something "less far fetched, that could happen to actual teenage girls" in Marianne's words.

It's hopeless. Quite apart from the fact that I can't imagine a Tallulah who allows herself to be constrained by what she's told is sensible behaviour, I'm too distracted to work. Beth does seem better, but I'm still reeling from the shock of seeing her have that fit yesterday evening. Plus, whenever I think about Mum and Dad coming home, my excitement builds, my heart racing with anticipation.

Beth is discharged around three, and Aunt Em

comes to collect us. Once we're home, Beth goes up to rest in her room. Amy, Meg and I creep around the house, trying to make as little noise as possible. Aunt Em starts sorting through her things. It's weird to imagine Mum and Dad being here, in their room. Over the past three months, Aunt Em has kind of made it her own. And Dad has never slept here at all.

Once Beth is settled, my thoughts turn to Lateef. I can't wait to tell him about Mum and Dad coming home tomorrow – and of course he needs to know about Beth's overnight stay in hospital too.

I message him about meeting up, but am too impatient to wait for a reply, so I fly across the road hoping he'll be in.

He is. In fact, he answers the door.

"I've been dying to see you," I gabble, bursting into the hall. "Did you get my message?"

"Yes, what's up?"

"A million things," I tell him, dragging him up the stairs to his room. "And all of them since yesterday."

"Oh, right," he says, rubbing the back of his head. "Actually, there was something I wanted to talk to you about too."

I give him a close look. Usually he's irrepressibly cheerful, but now he looks weighed down by troubles, his shoulders hunched and his jaw set in a grim line.

"Are you OK?" I ask.

"Fine." He manages a smile, sitting down on his couch. "Tell me what's been happening," he says.

"It's Beth. Actually it was awful," I explain, sitting down next to him. "She was so ill she had a fit and had to go to hospital."

Lateef's head jerks up. "Is she all right?"

"Yes, she's fine again now and back at home. The doctors say it was probably a virus and her temperature just went too high and that's why she had the seizure. They're doing some more tests but . . . but yesterday evening I had to call an ambulance to the house. I'm surprised you didn't see it outside."

Lateef shakes his head. "I was out with Uncle Jim," he says, his eyes full of concern. "How horrible."

"It was really scary."

"I bet," Lateef says. "Poor Beth, is she really OK?"

"I really think she is," I say, trying to reassure him. "I mean the doctors wouldn't let her out of hospital if she wasn't." I pause for breath. "But that isn't the only thing. We also found out yesterday that Mum's coming home tomorrow and *guess what?* She's bringing Dad with her." I beam at Lateef.

"That's brilliant," Lateef says. "I'm really pleased

for you. And it'll be great to see your mum again. And to meet your dad."

He's still smiling, but it's like the light has gone out in his eyes. I stare at him, the realization finally dawning that something *is* wrong.

"What's the matter?" I ask, leaning forward and touching his hand.

Lateef meets my gaze, his big brown eyes full of feeling. I've never met anyone with such an expressive face as Lateef. Impulsively I give his hand a squeeze. Lateef holds my fingers briefly, then lets go with a sigh.

My mobile rings. Meg. I answer, still looking at Lateef. "Aunt Em wants you to go to the corner shop and get some bread. OK?"

"Sure." I ring off and stand up. "I have to go down the road, Lateef," I explain. "I'll be back in a bit or . . . or d'you want to come with?"

"I . . ." He hesitates, then squares his shoulders. "There's something I need to tell you first."

I frown, leaning forward again. "What *is* it?" I ask. "Is it Uncle Jim?" A thought strikes me. "Or is it news from your home . . . your original home?"

"No." Lateef lowers his head. Outside, a passing car beeps its horn angrily. Then silence descends again. A beat passes as I wait for him to speak. When he does his voice is so low that I can hardly hear him. "It's you."

"Me?" I stare at him. "What have I done now?"

Lateef says nothing. I wrack my brains trying to work out why he might be upset with me. Then I remember the tension between us yesterday.

"Is it because of what happened at the picnic?" I ask. "I'm sorry if I was mean. I was just a bit embarrassed when you asked me that question about what I most wanted. It's not your fault and it's not that I'm ashamed of it, but when you tell people you want to be a writer lots of them think you're being really pretentious, so—" I shrug. "I felt weird about you asking me in front of everyone, and I was embarrassed and rude. I'm sorry."

"It's not that." Lateef looks up again and, to my horror, his eyes are bright with unshed tears. "It's how . . . how I feel about you. The way I think you feel about me." He gazes at me, urging me to understand.

Which I don't.

"What do you mean?" I ask. "What way?" I'm trying to sound light and jokey, but I can hear the sharp edge to my voice.

"I love you," Lateef says.

We stare at each other.

"Er, I know," I say, feeling bewildered. "Me too, like you're the brother I've never had, but we don't need to go around talking about it, do we?"

Lateef shakes his head. "No, that's what I'm trying to say . . . I love you, but *not* like a brother. I love you like. . ." He trails off, either from an inability to find the words to express himself or in horror at the shock that must be written all over my face.

"*What?*" I say, stupidly, my head spinning.

"I love you," Lateef says again. "That's it. I'm *in* love with you."

The words drop like acid on my skin. A single word roils up inside me, expressing everything that I feel.

Everything I know I will ever feel.

"No," I say. "I'm so sorry. *No*."

We stare at each other for a second, then Lateef's face floods with humiliation.

"I think you should go," he says.

I don't know how to argue. What to say. I don't want to leave like this.

My cheeks burn as I stand. "Lateef. . .?"

He doesn't look up. I walk over to the door, my stomach churns.

"Lateef, please."

Across the room, he jams on his headphones.

I have no choice but to make my way down the stairs and out of the house, feeling more alone than I've ever felt in my life.

Chapter 8

Almost twenty-four hours after my conversation with Lateef and I've neither seen, spoken with nor messaged him. It feels weird. Worse, it feels *wrong*. He's my best friend. We've seen each other almost every day since we met. When we aren't spending time with each other, we're chatting or messaging. And now, nothing.

Part of me wants to march over there and demand that we talk. But I have no idea what I'd say.

It still doesn't feel real that he said he's in love with me. Has he always felt like that? Why didn't he say something before? No, never mind that. Why on earth did he have to spoil everything by saying it at all? Our friendship was perfect and now he's gone and thrown a bomb in it.

I haven't told anyone. Partly from embarrassment, but also because everyone at home is totally preoccupied with their own stuff. Mum and Dad are due home in just a couple of hours and, when she hasn't been fussing over Beth, Aunt Em has been busy packing. Beth herself seems miles better, though her face is still pale and she doesn't have much of an appetite. She's spent the day resting in her bedroom, under strict instructions not to overexert herself.

Despite the fact that the doctors weren't able to identify whatever made her ill, Amy is convinced she's got glandular fever. Apparently Katy Brown had it last year and says all the symptoms match. Meanwhile Meg has been tidying and baking in anticipation of Mum and Dad coming back.

I still can't write my story for Teen Spiral. Perhaps I'm just too excited. I keep sitting down at my laptop but the words will not come. It's past five p.m. when I drift downstairs to the kitchen. Meg is taking a tray of cupcakes out of the oven, her rosy cheeks more flushed than usual.

"Don't touch," she snaps as I come over. "They need icing."

"Whatever." I veer away, towards the fruit bowl.

"Who wants one of your stupid cakes anyway?"

Meg straightens up. "Sorry," she says. "I'm just nervous."

"It's only Mum and Dad," I say, taking an apple. "They'll be so pleased to get back they won't care about a bunch of cupcakes."

"Not about that," Meg says with a sigh. "I need to talk to them about . . . about the courses I've been looking at."

I stare at her. "Lateef says working with kids is really hard work," I say. I'm still hoping that I can find a way of convincing Meg to see that she'll regret studying to be a nanny, that she'd be much better suited training to be a designer or a stylist.

Meg looks away.

"Why do you need to talk to Mum and Dad so urgently anyway? I mean, it's still only July. You don't have to start thinking about college applications until we're back at school."

Meg says nothing, just bites her lip.

I don't know what else to say to her. I feel too raw over Lateef to argue any more. It's like it was with Amy. A disagreement isn't worth losing a sister over.

I let out a long, heavy sigh. Meg tucks a loose strand of hair behind her eyes.

"Speaking of Lateef, where is he?" she asks. "I thought he'd be over today to see Beth – you did tell him she was ill when you went over yesterday, didn't you?"

"I did." I hesitate. I want to tell her what happened between us, but somehow it's too private, too awkward to explain. "I don't know where Lateef is," I say. "Are you going to see Aiden again?

"No," Meg says. "He's OK, but I'm not really interested."

"Right." I leave Meg placing her cakes on the cooling rack and wander back upstairs. As I reach my room, my phone pings with a message.

It's from Lateef.

On way to airport, going away for rest of summer. Better that way. Sorry about everything. L.

I sink on to my bed, studying his words. He's going away – because of me.

I scroll to his number, but it rings and rings with no answer and no way to leave a voicemail. So I message him.

Where are you going? I'll miss you. Hope you have a great time.

I hesitate, then send a second message which asks what I really want to know.

Can we still be friends?

There's no reply.

I've put out fresh towels and changed two sets of bed linen, and now I'm lying on my bed, thinking about Lateef again. Mum and Dad are due back any minute. Meg has showered and is drying her hair in our room. I still can't confide in her. I'm not sure if I could even put how I feel into words. Mostly I'm confused.

Confused and upset.

"Jo?" Beth calls from the landing.

I wander out. She's dressed in an old T-shirt and sweatpants, a smile on her pale face. "Are you coming downstairs with me? Mum and Dad will—"

As she speaks, the key sounds in the door. Her eyes widen. Downstairs, Amy and Meg squeal in unison.

"Daddy!" Amy's cry pierces the air.

I hold my breath. Beth grips my arm, her eyes glistening. "Come on."

I let her go first. Mum meets her halfway down the stairs with a big hug and a smile up at me. "Come on, Beth, you and Dad can be convalescents together in the living room."

They disappear down the stairs. I follow slowly, listening to Dad's gruff voice soften as he tells Beth how sorry he is to have been away and kept Mum away while she was in hospital. I reach the hall in time to see Amy virtually dragging Dad into the living room, everyone else following behind.

It feels surreal to have Dad back, to know that he is here, really here. I wander into the living room. Mum is by the door. She squeezes my arm. Meg is next to her, beaming at Dad. Beth is already on the sofa, Amy beside her, patting the seat next to her for Dad to sit down. They're all talking, laughing, looking up at him.

Dad. He's standing in the middle of the room, gazing at me. He looks even older and thinner and greyer than he did on Skype.

"Oh, Jo," he says. "My Jo. I've missed you so much."

And before I even know I'm going to move, I'm in his arms and bawling my eyes out.

A little later and everything is settling down. Dad and Beth have both been packed off upstairs to rest and Mum and Meg are preparing some food for supper. I wander into the living room, where Aunt Em is sipping a glass of wine, and Amy is curled up on the sofa with her sketchbook.

"Ah, Josephine," Aunt Em says, putting down her glass. "There's something I need to tell you."

I sit down opposite her.

"Beth is doing well and your parents are back now," Aunt Em explains, "so . . . so I've decided to go ahead and book my holiday to Europe."

I look up. "That's wonderful," I say. At last some good news. A holiday is just what I need: something to look forward to *and* a way to get my mind off Lateef. Maybe once we've both had some time away from home there'll be a way for us to build back our friendship again. "When do we leave, Aunt Em?"

Silence. Aunt Em is staring at me, an expression of confusion on her face. Out of the corner of my eye I see Amy looking up from her phone.

"Aunt Em?" I ask, suddenly uncertain.

Aunt Em coughs. "Er, Josephine, the fact is that . . . well, I've decided that Amy will be the best companion. She's young, but she's very capable."

"Oh." The blood pulses against my temples. Amy watches us.

"I know you've run a number of errands for me over the past few months," Aunt Em goes on, "but you have to admit there've been quite a few disasters:

the stain on my silk cushion, the spilled tray at my cocktail party, that glass of water at Easter—"

"It's fine," I lie, not wanting to hear more.

"And Amy has a real feel for what I need," Aunt Em says. "She's got a great eye and she understands my wardrobe and how I like to keep things and . . . well, Josephine, let's face it, you really have no interest in clothes or jewellery, do you?"

I glance at Amy, who looks away, her cheeks scarlet. I turn back to Aunt Em, disappointment coursing through me.

"You're quite right, Aunt Em." I glance at Amy who is still staring down at the floor, clearly mortified. In spite of my disappointment, my heart goes out to her. This isn't her fault. "Amy is the better choice," I say, trying to keep my voice light and cheerful. "It makes sense to take her. It's totally fine."

Amy looks up at me and I nod to emphasize what I've just said, pressing my lips firmly together so that she doesn't see how upset I am. I make an excuse and head upstairs, tears trickling down my face for the second time in two hours.

I lie on my bed, feeling utterly humiliated as I imagine the summer ahead: Lateef won't be here. Our friendship is destroyed anyway. Amy will be off in Europe. Meg will be looking after the little Gardiner boys and reading up on college courses. The next five weeks stretch ahead of me, dull and boring. For the first time I wonder if maybe I should have been more open to the idea of going out with Lateef. Perhaps if I love him as much as I do as a friend, I could fall in love with him too?

I sit up and lean back against the pillows. No, I'll be fine here, getting on with my writing and spending time with Beth – and with Mum and Dad.

A tear trickles down my face.

"Jo?" It's Mum in the doorway, her forehead creased with a frown.

She sits beside me and wipes the tear from my cheek. "I'm so sorry about the holiday with Aunt Em – I know you were hoping she'd take you with her. Amy's worried that you're upset." She gives me a rueful smile. "Which you clearly are. In fact I think Amy's anxious that you might be angry with her, but this really isn't her—"

"I'm not angry with Amy," I interrupt, swallowing down a sob. "Not at all. I totally get it. Amy is a better choice than me. Plus she deserves it – she's worked really hard looking after Aunt Em. I always complain.

And Amy actually enjoys all that stuff Aunt Em's into." I draw in a breath, big and shaky.

"So you're not crying about the trip?"

"Not really," I say, looking straight at Mum as the truth lands like a stone in my guts. "It's . . . it's Lateef."

Mum takes my hand. "Oh, Jo. You two had a row?"

I shake my head. "Much worse than that." I stare at my lap, unsure how to tell her. "He – he says he loves me, is *in* love with me." My lips tremble. "He's mad. Or I am. I don't know. I just know that I've lost my best friend."

Mum studies my face. "Oh, my darling. I did wonder about his feelings."

"Did you? Amy said something once too." I make a face. "I didn't. I thought we were fine being friends. Oh, Mum, do you think I should try and go out with him? It would be better than not seeing him at all."

Mum gives me a sad smile. "I don't think you can force yourself to love anyone. That sells both of you short." She hesitates. "May I be honest with you?"

I nod.

"All right." She pats my hand. "I like Lateef very much, and I think you are wonderful friends. But I don't think you two are really suited, not as romantic partners anyway. You're just so alike . . . *too* alike: impulsive and . . . well, both of you can be extremely hot-headed."

"But—"

"You're *friends*," Mum says firmly. "Great friends. And when you get to my age you'll realize just how rare and precious true friendship is." She smiles again. "I'm sure when Lateef's had time to think everything through he'll realize for himself what good friends you are and how he doesn't want to lose that."

"Really?" I ask. Mum nods and, for the first time in days, I let myself feel hopeful.

"Now come on," Mum says. "I want your help in the kitchen. Tonight we're going to have a special meal to celebrate Beth being well and Dad being home."

"OK," I say.

Mum sighs. "Remember that it's the sad times that help you appreciate when things are good."

I smile. "Next you'll be telling me that what doesn't kill you makes you stronger."

"Also true." Mum laughs. "But as a family we have plenty to be grateful for."

I follow her downstairs. Mum's right, of course.

But no matter how much I tell myself to be thankful for what I have, the prospect of a whole summer without my best friend at my side sends my heart plummeting into my shoes.

Part Four

Autumn

Chapter 1

It's the first week of September, the new school year is about to start and everyone except me seems to be getting on with their lives.

It's been hard getting through the past few weeks without Lateef, though the fact he is abroad makes it a little easier. At least there's no risk of bumping into him on Fishtail Lane or at the few social gatherings I've been invited to.

I'm still trying to write and getting nowhere. With each idea I've completed a few paragraphs . . . then lost interest. For a start I can't find anyone interesting to write about. Certainly nobody as cool as Tallulah Templeton. I miss her and her wild adventures. Marianne's idea of more grown-up fiction that "teens could feel might really happen to them" seems to me more like a way of confining people my age, putting them in a box and allowing them to play there, but not to risk going out into the world. It's patronizing.

Worse, it's dull.

So here I am, sitting at the kitchen table in front of my computer while the sun streams on to the back garden where Mum and Beth are pottering about, pointing at flowers and Beth's little vegetable patch. She sees me watching and gives me a cheerful wave. She tells us that she's feeling better each day. To my mind she still looks very pale and seems to get tired far too easily. I know Mum and Dad are anxious about her too. At least they're not worrying about money so much any more: Mum has just started working in the HR department of a local company. It's only part time, but better paid than her old full-time job – and, best of all, Mum's really enjoying it.

I give up on my story and fetch myself a glass of water. It's times like these when I really wish I could call or see Lateef. I haven't heard from him directly since he declared his love over a month ago – though he's posting on social media several times a day from the amazing places he's visiting on holiday.

I wander into the living room where Meg is lying on the sofa, studying her phone intently.

"I'm bored," I say.

"Uh-huh." Meg clearly isn't listening.

"The kitchen's on fire," I say, to test her out.

"Uh-huh." A short pause, then Meg looks up at me, squinting a frown. "What?"

"Forget it," I say with a sigh, sinking on to the arm of the nearest chair. "What are you doing?"

"Nothing," she says.

"Are you looking at nanny jobs?" I ask. Meg hasn't talked to me about her plans to work in childcare since the day Mum and Dad came home weeks ago. She's spoken to them though; I've seen them huddled together, serious expressions on their faces.

"No."

"University courses?" I persist. "Because there's still months and months before you'd have to apply to Nanny University or wherever."

Meg casts an irritated sideways glance at me. "Go away," she says.

Rolling my eyes, I head upstairs.

I flop on to my bed and tug on my headphones. While I listen to music, I scroll through Amy's

Facebook posts. These are carefully put together for Mum and Dad's benefit:

Got to Rome yesterday. There is lots of traffic and it is very hot. Today we went to a famous fountain.

In Florence where there's a big cathedral and some of the streets smell bad. My hotel room has a balcony.

And my personal favourite, from the start of her holiday:

Paris is hot. There is a big river and the Eyeful Tower. I saw a cat with three legs and lots of tourists.

Smiling to myself, I open up Amy's Instagram and Snapchat posts, which is where her more authentic experiences are to be found. Today she's put up a picture of a row of brightly coloured bicycles on the banks of a river, the water reflecting as dancing light on their spokes. She doesn't say where the picture is taken, just a couple of hashtags: #pretty and #bicycles. She's already had over a-hundred-and-seventy likes. I sigh. It does look amazing. I have to hope that my time to travel the world will come one day, even if I haven't yet figured out how to make it happen.

A light knock on the door, just audible over the music pumping through my headphones. I look up as it opens.

I gasp. Lateef is standing there, his hair cut very short. My stomach lurches with the shock of seeing him. I sit up quickly and tug off my headphones.

"Hey, Jo March. What's up?" He grins.

"You're back." I study his face, my heart pounding. Why is he here? To confess his feelings all over again? No, surely not: he's leaning against the doorframe, completely relaxed, and the expression in his eyes reveals nothing more complicated than pleasure at seeing me. There's no trace of the unhappy boy who said he was in love with me all those weeks ago.

"Yes, I'm back. Well spotted," he says with a grin. He saunters across the room and sits opposite me, on Meg's bed. "Got home a couple of hours ago actually. Had a great time, but. . ." He hesitates. "But before I tell you about that I need to say something else."

I gulp. He *is* going to talk about his feelings. Oh, no. I don't want to hear another declaration of love. I can't bear the idea of rejecting him again – of hurting my best friend.

"What's that?" I say lightly. "How you lazed your way around Europe?"

"No." Lateef hesitates again. A shadow passes over his expressive face. I brace myself for whatever is coming next. "It's two things really. First, I'm sorry I haven't been in touch. I missed your crazy messages."

"Yeah," I say, with feeling. Meaning "me too", though not wanting quite to actually acknowledge that I've missed him at all. "I didn't expect you to be in touch after. . ." I trail off. The words "after the way you left" hang in the air between us.

Lateef nods. "I was upset," he says.

I look down. This is it. He's about to tell me he loves me again.

"Hey, get over yourself, Jo March." He laughs. "Don't worry, I'm not upset any more."

"Oh," I say, filled with surprise – and relief. "Er . . . good."

"Yeah, so . . . though I hate to admit you were right, I've realized that you were." He wrinkles his nose. "You and me – we're better off as friends. *So* much better off in fact."

I stare at him. "*Really*?" I ask eventually.

"Totally," he says. "I think a part of me knew it from the start, but I was such a mess when I left. . . Anyway, gradually things started to change. And meeting up with Amy helped too."

"Amy?" I raise my eyebrows, a funny feeling in the

pit of my stomach. "She never mentioned she saw you. When was this?"

"I asked her not to," Lateef admits. "You know, she's a smart kid. We met up when we were both in Rome a couple of weeks back. She guessed how I felt about. . ." He looks away. "Whatever, she's cleverer than you think."

I nod, thinking back to the morning after Lateef and I had our fight over the Manning Plains tickets, when Amy told me Lateef liked me.

"So what did she say?" I ask, curious in spite of myself.

"I dunno, just stuff about how smart you are, how important writing is to you. . . She said how she admires that you know what you want and you're really focused on achieving it."

My jaw drops. "*Amy* said that?" It's hard to imagine her saying anything so positive about me. "She'd never say that to my face."

"Maybe not," Lateef acknowledges. "But she still looks up to you."

"Oh."

"Anyway, we talked about you and how amazing you are, and afterwards I realized that you are – you're great – but that you and I wouldn't be great together. I'll never be able to understand how you feel about writing." He leans forward. "But I know that one day you'll make it as a writer, Jo, and I'd like to be there, cheering you on." He grins. "You're the first person I want as a friend, and the *last* person I'd want for a girlfriend."

"Thanks, Lateef." I laugh, mostly with relief, though there's also a sadness in there too – not about me and Lateef, just a sense that life won't ever be quite the same again. . .

Lateef laughs too. "You're my best friend, Jo, like my sister, like how you said I was your brother. At least you *were* my best friend before the summer." He spreads his arms and leans forward and the sunlight through the window glints off his sleek, dark hair. "Can we go back to that?"

I study him. We can't go back. I know that. I'll always remember how he felt about me and it will always change our friendship. But maybe that doesn't have to be a bad thing. Maybe getting the romance question out of the way now means that we'll be able to be even better friends in the future.

Whatever, the truth is that I've missed him and the summer's been worse for not having him around and now that a new school year is about to start, maybe it's exactly the right time for us to make up and move forward.

Our eyes meet. "I've missed you too," I say gruffly. "And even if it has taken you weeks I guess you got there in the end so, yeah, if it means so much to you, I suppose we can be friends."

We are both smiling now, grinning like idiots.

"Best friends the sequel," I say with a chuckle. "Here we come."

Chapter 2

Lateef and I go downstairs together and within minutes it's like he's never been away. Amy still isn't home, of course. She's not due back for another few days. But Meg and Beth make a big fuss of him and when I introduce him to Dad, who's taken over Mum's vegetable gardening as a way of building up his strength, Lateef really turns on the charm.

"It's so great to meet you, Mr March," he says, his eyes merry and his grin huge. "I've heard so much about you."

"And I you," Dad says, straightening up from his tomato plants to shake hands. "Nice to have another bloke about the place."

"Glad to hear you're making a good recovery. When are you going back to work?" Lateef asks.

I give a tiny gasp under my breath as the sun emerges from one cloud and disappears swiftly behind another. None of us have asked this question since Dad got home. I don't think any of us could bear to. Now I feel a gust of chilly air creep up my spine.

Dad hesitates, then turns to me. "Actually, I was just discussing this with your mum, Jo." He pauses. "I'm not going back. At least, I'm not going abroad again."

"Really?" I dart forward and envelope him in a gigantic hug. He feels so frail still, far thinner than I remember from when he went away last year.

"Really." Dad pats my back. "I was going to tell everyone when Amy got home, but it's not a secret."

I pull back and look at him. "What will you do instead?" I ask.

He grins. "I'll be kept busy, don't worry. I'm going to carry on recuperating for the rest of this year then start looking for a permanent job in January. There's a lot of work for a consultant with knowledge of the Middle East in the charity sector."

I nod, my eyes prickling with emotion. I glance at Lateef, who smiles.

"That's great news," he says quietly, and I nod. It is. It really, really is.

Later, while Mum and Dad potter in the garden, we all sit slumped in the sitting room, digesting the good news. "I wonder where Dad will end up working?" Beth muses from her perch on the living-room sofa.

"I wonder that about all of us," I add. "Where will *we* end up? The world is so big. And I want to see every last bit of it."

Meg laughs. "Me too. Some of it, at least."

"I'd be happy staying right here," Beth says quietly.

"Hey." Lateef sits up straight. He's in the big armchair opposite me and Beth, Meg lounging on the floor in front of the TV. "Let's say what we all want when we're older. Like, proper dreams and ambitions and . . . and nobody's allowed to laugh at anybody else's." He looks around at each of us, his expression equal parts amused and challenging.

We all glance at each other and then nod. It's kind of hard to resist Lateef. "You first," I say.

"Sure." Lateef sits up. "I realized this over the summer: what I really want is to be a musician, a guitarist." He turns to me. "And before you point out that I didn't practise the piano enough, so why would it be different with the guitar, that's exactly what I'm saying ... that I'm going to start lessons next week and really work at it, a couple of hours every evening." He sits back in the armchair, beaming. "I bet that's what you want too, Beth – being a pianist, I mean. Isn't it?"

We all look at Beth. She gulps. "Actually, I love the piano but what I would really like is to work as a carer. Maybe a nurse. But I'd stay at home for the training and do it all so I can look after Mum and Dad if Dad gets ill again or . . . or when they get really old."

Lateef nods.

"That's perfect, Beth," I say.

Meg stares at me. "How come it's OK for Beth to want to care for people who are sick, but stupid for me to want to look after children?"

I turn to her. Is she still upset about this? I thought we'd moved on ages ago.

"Is that what you want to do, Meg?" asks Lateef, clearly trying to avoid us having a row. "Be a teacher?"

"No, I want to look after younger kids, like I do with the Gardiner boys," Meg says. She throws me an irritated glance. "But Jo here thinks that's stupid."

"I *don't* think it's stupid," I say. "It's just, well, if

you must bring it up again, then Beth looking after people makes total sense, but you've always been so into styles and designs. I always imagined that after A-levels you'd go to art school, or study design at uni. I mean, whatever you choose is fine, but have you actually thought about what you really want?"

"Can you hear how patronizing you sound?" Meg's voice rises. "What gives you the right to decide what makes sense for anyone else? It's so typical of you, Jo, to think you know best. You can be so *arrogant* sometimes."

The atmosphere in the room tenses. Beth stares down at her lap, refusing to make eye contact with either of us. In contrast Lateef is frowning, glancing from me to Meg.

"Hey, come on, this wasn't supposed to cause a row," he says.

"It hasn't *caused* one," Meg says, a bitter note to her voice. "Jo's been on my case for months about what she *thinks* I should do, instead of actually *listening* to what I *want* to do."

I sigh, feeling aggrieved. Mum's words, unbidden, flash into my head:

Maybe because you feel so passionately about writing, you've assumed Meg feels the same about dress designing?

"So tell us, Meg," Lateef says in his most soothing voice. "Tell us what you want to do."

"I want to be a nanny." Meg looks around at each of us in turn. "I've thought and thought about it. And it's perfect for me – I love looking after kids." She pauses. "I mean, I love fashion too, but in the same way that Beth loves playing the piano. And just as it wouldn't suit Beth to have to perform in front of people, it wouldn't suit me to have to sit down and draw designs and work out how to make clothes."

I stare at her. I'd never thought about it like that . . . that to Meg, maybe those things felt like a chore.

"It doesn't mean I can't carry on dressing with style. . ." She grins in my direction. "And helping you do that too, Jo, 'cos you certainly need it."

"Whatever." I make a face at her.

"That's just like how I'm going to carry on playing the piano," Beth adds timidly. "Because I like to do that, for myself."

"Mmmn." Lateef raises his eyebrows. "Maybe not everyone's like you, Jo, ready to risk it all for a dream."

"I don't think of writing stories as a dream," I say. "It's the only thing I want to do. That and travel the world having adventures and getting ideas for my next book."

Lateef grins. "Which I can totally see you doing."

"Me too," Beth says, a soft smile on her lips. "You've got a great dream, Jo. You don't need to worry about anyone else's."

She's right.

I glance at Meg. "I'm sorry if I dissed your nanny thing," I say gruffly. "I think you'll be great at it. And if it's what you want you should go for it."

Meg sighs. "I'm sorry I said you were patronizing and arrogant."

"Jeez," says Lateef. "Are we still talking about this?"

"Shut up," the three of us chorus, as in unison we each reach for the nearest cushion and chuck it across the room at him.

Chapter 3

It's two days before the autumn term at school starts and Ringstone, like most of England, is sweltering in an unexpected September heatwave. Meg, Beth and I are lazing in the garden hoping to catch a waft of non-existent breeze. Amy will be home from her travels any minute – Mum and Dad have sent a text to say they're on their way back from the airport.

I'm on my phone, on Twitter, composing a tweet to Rowena Riddell. She won't remember me from the book signing – but I'm desperate for some advice. The deadline for my story for Teen Spiral is creeping ever closer and I still haven't written a word. In the end I decide on:

Am a big fan and a writer too. Met you at Ringstone

signing back in Jan. Any advice for writer's block? Getting desperate! Thanks!

I post the tweet and lie back on the lawn. Meg and Beth have claimed a rickety lounger each but I prefer the patchy grass in the shade of the bushes.

I close my eyes, half asleep. Over the past few weeks I've got used to the house without Amy and all her giggly friends. What will it be like having her back? Under my fingers the earth feels dry and warm.

"She's here!" Beth cries. "Amy!"

I open my eyes. Meg springs up from her lounger. She and Beth are already hurrying across the grass. I follow them over to the patio.

Amy is standing, framed by the kitchen door. My jaw drops.

She's transformed. In place of her girly blonde curls is a sleek, expensively cut bob. And instead of the flouncy pink dress she departed in she is wearing a fitted white T-shirt, grey cut-offs and a soft, silk jacket the exact colour of her eyes.

"Wow!" Meg gasps, tracing her hand along the sleeve of Amy's jacket as she pulls her into a hug. "You look amazing."

"You look so grown up, Amy," Beth says, offering her own, more timid embrace.

"You look like a mini version of Aunt Em," I add, kissing her cheek.

Old Amy would have got riled at this.

New Amy simply shields her face from the sun with her hand and smiles. It's strange. Beth is right, she *does* look older. But it's not just the clothes, it's the whole way she's carrying herself.

"This direct sunshine is *'streemly* bad for your skin," Amy says with such an authoritative air that I almost burst out laughing. "Let's go inside."

She turns on her heel and Meg, Beth and I troop after her into the kitchen.

"Did you have a good time?" Meg asks, sitting down at the kitchen table and motioning Amy to sit opposite.

"Oh, yes." Amy's grin widens and for a second she looks like a little girl again. "I saw . . . just *amazing* things. It was *brilliant!*"

A little stab of envy pierces me. I open my mouth to say something sarcastic about Amy's powers of description, but then I close it again. Amy sinks gracefully into a kitchen chair.

"What was the *best* thing about the trip?" Beth asks breathlessly, slipping into the chair next to Meg's.

Amy smiles. For a moment I think she's going to

say something mean about how great it was being away from all of us – but maybe that says more about me than her. After all, getting some space apart from my family has been such a long-standing desire of mine it's easy to assume everyone else feels the same way too.

"The best thing," Amy says, widening her eyes for theatrical effect. "Was the day we went to a catwalk show in Paris."

"*Seriously?*" I burst out laughing. "You went all the way to France and Italy and the best bit was watching a load of models prancing about on a runway."

Beth and Meg stiffen, no doubt expecting to see old Amy now: a firework about to explode with righteous indignation at me for teasing her.

Instead Amy leans back, simply raising a languid eyebrow in my direction. "*Actually,* the show was in this amazing, modern building on the banks of the Seine. Beforehand, Aunt Em and I went to the Louvre and looked at the paintings, and after the show everyone went for drinks on the river – including all these designers Aunt Em knows and people wearing bright colours and clothes with feathers, like birds. The views were incredible and the sun was shining and Aunt Em even let me have a sip of her champagne, which was the first time I ever had any." Amy wrinkles her nose. "Not that I liked it, but the day overall was brilliant."

I nod, feeling uncomfortably like I've been put in my place.

Out of the corner of my eye I spot Mum and Dad in the kitchen doorway.

"The next day was when Aunt Em bought me this jacket." Amy rubs the soft grey-blue silk between her fingers. "Isn't it the most lovely colour?"

"It is, Amy." Mum exchanges a worried glance with Dad. "Your aunt has been very generous."

Dad grimaces. He's probably wondering how on earth he and Mum will be able to pay Aunt Em back for the jacket.

"She was," Amy acknowledges. "But she said she was happy to buy it – as a thank you for me being so helpful." She looks through the open door out to the garden. "Wow, it's as hot here as it was in Italy."

Mum clears her throat. "Are you hungry, sweetheart?"

"Ooh, yes." Amy nods eagerly, looking again, briefly, like the little girl she was when she left. "Is there any cake?"

"There is." Mum laughs. "I made a chocolate sponge with raspberry icing. Your favourite."

"Thanks, Mum." Amy beams as Mum fills the kettle with water.

Amy produces her presents – a large box of chocolates for me and little silver earrings for Meg and Beth. My phone pings with an alert. I glance down. Could this be a response from Rowena Riddell? Some advice about dealing with writer's block?

But it's just someone from school liking my Instagram pic of the spider's web spread across the rose bush in our back garden.

Dad cooks a special dinner in honour of Amy's return home. There's a big lasagne with salad and a trifle – or more of Mum's cake – for pudding. We're just getting to the end of the meal and Dad is looking tired, as he often does if he's been standing for too long. Mum expresses concern and Meg quickly shoos them both out of the kitchen saying the four of us will clear up.

"Including Amy," she adds firmly.

Mum and Dad leave, while Beth starts gathering the plates and Meg and I begin washing and drying up. Amy deals with all the leftovers, covering the lasagne and trifle and putting them in the fridge.

She fits the scant remains of the chocolate cake back in its tin, then turns to face us all. "I made a will while I was away," she says

I stare at her, the plate I'm drying forgotten in my hands.

"What?" Meg frowns, flicking a soap sud from her wrist.

"Why?" I ask.

"Are you sick?" Beth adds, leaning forward with an anxious frown.

"No, silly." Amy rolls her eyes. "But Aunt Em was talking about *her* will and I just wanted all my off. . . my aff. . . all my stuff in order. I mean, it's not an official thing, but it's written down and signed."

"*Seriously,* Amy?" I snort, rolling my eyes.

"*Jo,*" Meg says absently. "How many times? You sound like a man when you make that sound."

Amy shoots me a withering glance. "So. . ." she continues. "I've left everything to Mum and Dad, *obviously.* But I thought you'd like to know that I've made separate special *bisects* for you three."

"You mean *bequests,*" I snigger.

"Whatever." Amy draws herself up. "I've given Meg any of my clothes she wants, except the pink pom-pom jumper which has got to go to Katy, who can also have my necklaces and other jewellery."

"OK," Meg says uncertainly. "You know your clothes won't fit me, right?"

"Then Beth can have my old dolls and those slippers with the satin bow that she likes."

I exchange a look with Beth, who, despite her love of her own old teddy bear, I'm pretty certain has no interest in Amy's discarded toys.

Beth smiles. "Thanks, Amy."

Looking pleased with herself, Amy turns to me. "And, Jo, you are getting my bedside lamp – the one with the shade that's wonky because you dropped it once – and also my laptop because I'm sorry I destroyed your story that time."

I meet Amy's eager eyes and, though part of me is desperate to tease her about her stupid bequests, I can't actually bring myself to do it. "Great," I say gruffly.

"That's sorted then," says Amy and leaves the kitchen.

"That girl is insane," Meg mutters.

I check my phone again. There's still no reply from my favourite author. Which means I still have no idea how to get past my writer's block – and that I am as stuck as ever trying to find a stupid story.

Chapter 4

I trudge reluctantly into school just as the bell rings.

The start of a new school year has never felt less appealing. For one thing it's my GCSE year, which means hard work and high expectations and having to study loads of stuff that doesn't interest me. On top of that, I'm going to have to face Sallie Gardiner and Zoe Carpenter, who I haven't seen since we got back from the festival and who have probably told half the school that I'm only friends with Lateef because he's rich.

To make matters worse, neither Meg nor Beth have made it into school today. Amy's here – she's just skipped past me, all smiles and giggles, with Katy and their other friends – but Beth isn't well enough.

"The doctor says she could do with a bit more time," Mum said. "She's not coming on quite as quickly as they would like."

As for Meg, she claimed this morning to be unwell herself, turning over in bed when I prodded her to get up. She's been huddled in secret conversations with Mum and Dad for the past week. I've asked what they're talking about, but Meg just keeps saying she's not ready to explain yet.

I don't know what she's up to, but I'm certain she's not ill. What's more, I'm also certain Mum and Dad know it. So why are they putting up with it?

And why is Meg shutting me out?

The bell rings as I make my way along the corridor to the hall. There's a full school assembly before our new form teachers take us off to our new form rooms and give us our timetables. I spot Amy on the end of a row as I pass. She's still deep in conversation with her friends and doesn't notice me.

Lateef waves as I get close to my own year. He's standing next to Tiny with Sallie Gardiner on the other side. I hesitate, then give them a friendly wave and drop into a seat a couple of rows back. I can't face Sallie right now. I keep my eyes on the stage, where the head is shuffling papers, adjusting the microphone on its stand.

"Aren't you going to say hello?"

I turn to find Zoe standing next to me, Sallie at her side. Lateef is still in his place a few rows ahead, chatting and laughing with Tiny.

"Oh," I say. "Er – hello."

"How come you didn't say hi just now?" asks Sallie. Then a look of fake comprehension comes over her face. "Oh my God. Were you *jealous*? Of me talking to Lateef?"

I frown. "I have no idea what. . ."

"She's really in denial, isn't she?" Zoe's lips curve into a sneer. "Poor Lateef."

"I was only *talking* to him," Sallie says with a roll of her eyes. "Jeez."

I stare at her, bewildered.

"It's not just her, it's that *younger* sister too," Zoe says, pointing in Amy's direction. I can see her blonde head close to Katy's dark one. "*That* one has *such* a crush on him. Ha! You know what, Sallie? If one sister doesn't get her hooks in him the other will."

"Shut up!" The words shoot out of me and I see a few people look around in surprise. My cheeks burn.

After a lifetime with three sisters I know enough about teasing to have learned that it's best ignored. But that's impossible. It's bad enough Zoe and Sallie being nasty to me, but no way will I put up with them picking on Amy.

Sallie flinches but Zoe smiles like she's won something.

"Looks like we touched a nerve," she says smugly.

"Leave me alone," I say coldly. "And leave Amy alone too."

The head taps the microphone on the stage and calls for everyone's attention.

"Please, be seated," he intones.

Zoe disappears, Sallie scuttling in her wake.

I sink back in my seat, listening to the head drone on and feeling more despondent than ever. What on earth just happened?

It's a long first day back. Thankfully I'm in a different form room from both Zoe and Sallie and can take a locker next to Lateef's without worrying about their mean comments.

I don't see either girl again until lunch break. They're in a different set for maths and science and, unlike me, aren't taking history.

Lateef also has different lessons from me for most of the morning. He seeks me out at the soup bar in the canteen at lunch break to tell me that this year's school play is going to be *My Fair Lady*.

"I just saw Mr Peterson putting up a poster," he tells me, grabbing a clutch of bread rolls. "You should audition, Jo, you'd be brilliant."

"Uh-huh." I'm only half listening, my attention mostly on Zoe across the room. She's chatting to Sallie and a few other girls from our year, pointing over at us. They all burst out laughing and I flush.

"What a cow," I mutter.

Lateef stops mid-story. He frowns. "Sorry?"

"Don't turn around," I say. "But it's Zoe Carpenter. She hates me, she's been saying. . ." I meet his gaze. "She's making stuff up about us, making out I'm jealous if you talk to anyone else. She's even saying *Amy* has a crush on you! How mad can you get?"

Lateef studies my face, a slow smile lighting his expression. "Amy *does* have a crush on me," he says, eventually.

"What?" I stare at him in shock, and then burst out laughing. "You certainly think a lot of yourself, Lateef. No way. She sees you like a brother. Like I do."

"Nope." Lateef tilts his head to one side. His smile

is still there, but there's a flicker of something else in his eyes. "That's how *you* see me, Jo March. But Amy has a crush. So does Zoe Carpenter, for that matter." He grins, stretching his arms above his head. "I can't help it, I'm just a natural babe magnet."

I roll my eyes. "Yeah, right." I fall silent, deep in thought. "You're wrong about Amy," I say eventually. "Whatever you might think, she finds you as annoying as the rest of us. But Zoe..." I hesitate. "Do you like her back?" I don't think I could bear it if Lateef started going out with that nightmare.

"No way." Lateef grins. "Tell you what. Let's go and sit with her. Smother her with niceness. We'll be so nice to her she'll have to get over herself."

Before I can protest, he's leading the way across the dining hall. I pick up my tray and follow. Zoe flushes as he nears the table and then she gathers herself and directs a big smile at Lateef, making space for him beside her. Me she ignores entirely.

"Rubbish being back, isn't it?" Lateef says cheerily, sitting down. The two girls opposite Zoe pick up their trays and hurry off, giggling to each other. "Did you go away anywhere nice in the holidays?" Lateef asks.

"France," she says, in a voice that is clearly striving

to sound casual. "Camping." She shrugs. "My older sister was *totally* annoying."

"Nightmare," Lateef says sympathetically. "Did you have to share a tent?"

"Yes *and* my dad made us walk to the shops for bread *every* day." Zoe rolls her eyes. "My sister made me do the talking. *So* embarrassing."

"Well at least your French will have improved," Lateef says with a grin.

"I suppose that is true," Zoe agrees with a giggle.

I sigh. I don't know how he does it – make everyone like him so easily. I sit down opposite them, marvelling at the change in Zoe's manner. All her hard angles and sneers are gone, leaving her soft and vulnerable.

Lateef's right; she *does* like him.

I almost feel sorry for her.

"Hey, Jo." It's Amy, breezing over. Even in her school uniform she seems older than before she went to Europe. She looks her usual, relaxed self and barely glances at Lateef. "Did you see the posters going up about *My Fair Lady* as the school play?"

"Mmm, Lateef mentioned it." I peer closely at my sister. Is that a touch of mascara on her eyelashes?

I tuck into the pasta on my plate, hiding a smile, as Lateef says hello to Amy before she flits away – then carries on chatting with Zoe. He leaves when the bell rings and Zoe is clearly so delighted by his attention that she even manages to smile a goodbye at me. She's certainly much nicer to me later on in our drama class.

Dad and Meg are in the garden, deep in conversation, when I get home.

"Hi!" I call out to them.

"Hi!" Dad replies. "How was the first day back?"

"Fine," I say. "Although I think this year is going to be intense. . ."

"Give us a minute," Dad says, "and then I want to hear all about it."

I hesitate. From the way Meg is fidgeting from foot to foot, she is clearly concerned about something.

"What are you guys talking about?" I ask.

Dad looks at Meg.

"You're not really ill, are you?" I glare at my sister. "What's going on?"

Meg remains tight-lipped – her expression annoyingly self-important,

"Oh, whatever." I stomp off.

I'm really losing patience with Meg and her endless secret chats.

I go up to our room and get out my laptop. I open up a page in Word and type the title for a new story: *Crush*.

I start writing about what happened today, changing all the names. To my amazement, the words flow out of me: Zoe's nasty comments at assembly in the morning; Lateef's suggestion that we sit with her; the way she looks at him; the way Lateef handles it all. I write about their feelings – at least, how I imagine them. And I write about myself: about the way my friendship with Lateef has changed over the summer and how maybe we're even closer now because we went through something hard and weird and have come out the other side.

"Jo?" I look up to find Dad standing in the doorway. The light is fading from the room. He flicks on the switch. I must have been writing for hours.

"You looked so absorbed earlier I didn't want to disturb you," he says. "So how was school?"

"Interesting," I say absently, still looking at my laptop. "I'm writing about some of it now."

Dad glances at my laptop with raised eyebrows. "What happened to the writer's block?"

I stare at the screen. The word count is telling me I've written almost nine-hundred words. That's more than I've managed all summer. It's not ready for Teen Spiral yet, but it's a start. I smile at Dad.

"Maybe I just needed to find something I wanted to write about." I suddenly remember Rowena Riddell's words from that signing.

Find a way of writing what you know.

I don't care any more that she didn't reply to me on Twitter. She already gave me brilliant advice, face to face, at the start of the year. I didn't understand it at the time but I do now:

It's fine to write about whatever you want – from your own experiences to action-paced fantasy dramas and everything in between. I certainly intend to try out lots of different genres and styles in the months and years to come. What really counts is writing from the heart, about what matters passionately to you, and finding the truth in those things. That way your stories will be real and powerful and meaningful, even when every single word is made up.

"I knew you'd get there." Dad smiles back. "I'll leave you to it – you can tell me about school later." He turns away.

"Actually, Dad, can I ask you something?"

Dad turns back.

"What's going on with Meg?" I ask. "She's been having these secret conversations with you for over a week. What's that about? Why wasn't she at school today? Why won't anyone talk to me?"

He hesitates. "You're right, Jo. It's time you knew. Come on."

Chapter 5

Dad leads the way into the living room, where Meg is on the sofa, staring out of the window. She seems lost in thought, looking vacantly round as Dad sits beside her.

My heart thuds as I ease myself into the armchair opposite. Dad clears his throat. He is still so much slighter than I remember before he went away – his face haggard and deep lines etched across his forehead.

"Meg," he says gently. "I think it's time to explain your plans to Jo."

Meg looks up at me. Her eyes are round with apprehension, their expression part anxious, part defiant.

There's a tense silence. I raise my eyebrows, trying to lighten the mood. "So go on, Meg. Are you eloping with that guy from the beach? Becoming a nun? Running away to—"

"I'm not going back to school," Meg says.

I glance at Dad in surprise. He and Mum have always been insistent we should make the most of our education. I can't believe he'd be happy for Meg to jack it all in.

"What d'you mean?" I ask, leaning forward. "You're getting a nanny job *now?*"

"No," Meg explains. "I mean I'm going to an FE college that does a really good childcare BTec alongside my A-levels. And they organize placements too. It'll set me up brilliantly to either get a job or maybe do a proper nanny diploma afterwards."

"Oh," I say. "Well, er, great. If that's what you really want."

"It is," Meg says. She glances at Dad.

"Mum and I have talked it over and considered all the options," Dad says. "At first I wanted Meg to stay where she was, where you're all together and settled, but Meg thinks – and Mum and I agree – that she'll be better off if she's able to focus on what she feels passionate about."

I nod, slowly. I've never really seen Meg's ambition to work with children as a passion before. It suddenly occurs to me that if Meg feels half as strongly about becoming a nanny as I do about becoming a writer, then I understand her better than I think. And, if our situations were reversed, then what I'd want from her is encouragement and support.

"That's brilliant, Meg," I say, beaming at her. "I'm so pleased you've found a course that'll help you do something you really want to do."

Meg blinks, clearly startled by my enthusiasm.

"So where's the college?" I go on. "Is it that big place on the edge of Ringstone?"

"No, er, it's, er, John Brooke College," Meg says. "It's actually quite a way from here."

"Giving you the perfect opportunity to do your coursework on the bus journey home." I chuckle. "You know, I thought you and Dad were going to tell me something *massive*. But this . . . it'll be a bit weird you not being at school, but I guess nothing else will really change that much."

Meg gulps. "Actually, it *will* change." She hesitates. "John Brooke College is in Manchester. I'll be living there as . . . as of this weekend."

My jaw drops. Is she serious? I look at Dad again. He's nodding.

"It's a big move and Meg's young to be making it, but she's sure that this is what she wants. Mum and I are fully behind her."

"It's the best course, Jo," Meg adds.

"She did really well to get on to it," Dad says with pride. "Got a bursary and everything."

My stomach flips over. Although Meg is older than me by fifteen months and two whole school years, I'd always somehow assumed that *I'd* be the first one to leave home. And yet here's Meg about to zoom off to another part of the country to make her dreams come true, just after Amy's spent nearly a month travelling around France and Italy, places *I've* always dreamed of exploring. It's like my sisters' lives are taking off – and I'm stuck here, in this crowded house with GCSEs that I don't want to take, at a school where I have hardly any friends and a story for Teen Spiral that *still* refuses to come together.

"I'll be staying with a friend of Aunt Em's about ten minutes' walk from the college," Meg says anxiously, her eyes fixed on mine. "The rent isn't very much and I should hopefully be able to pick up some babysitting work which. . ." She trails off. "Jo?"

"Wow, that's all just so... I mean it's brilliant. Clever you, Meg." I hope my voice doesn't sound as hollow as I feel. It's weird, ever since we moved to Ringstone I've chafed against sharing a room with Meg, but now... I don't know how to feel. Other than abandoned. Which is stupid. And unfair on Meg. I need to stop being so sorry for myself and be happy for her instead.

I glance at Dad. He's studying my face carefully.

"The money Mum and I are spending on Meg's rent," he says, "we're going to make sure we put some aside so we can help you, later, Jo. *All* of you."

I smile at him. "Of course, Dad, it's fine. I'm really pleased Meg's got it all so sorted."

Meg smiles, her expression full of relief. "Are you sure you don't mind, Jo? You won't miss me too much?"

"Miss you?" I grin. "Are you kidding? I'll have our room to myself at last!"

Two weeks pass and, as we head towards the end of September, the balmy summer air turns cooler. Meg is settling in at John Brooke College in Manchester and messages on a regular basis. Sounds like she's having a great time, making friends, enjoying the course and loving her lodgings at Aunt Em's friend's house. It all sounds so grown up. She feels very far away.

I miss her, sure, especially in the middle of the night when I wake and it feels weird to be in the dark of night without her breathing sounds across the room, but not as much as I might have imagined.

The day after Meg left I started writing about her leaving. Well, not just that, but about how close we are, in spite of being so different, and how I hadn't properly realized it until now. I didn't think I would have that much to say, but to my surprise I ended up with a few thousand words. I really hope I'm getting closer to something Marianne will like.

On the last Wednesday in September, I go to school with a spring in my step. I've decided – last minute – to audition for the school production of *My Fair Lady* that Lateef told me about on our first day back. I hadn't planned to get involved. I'd thought that I wanted to spend all my spare time writing – but since Meg left for Manchester I've realized that being open to other stuff is important too.

Plus I used to love acting out our old Rachel and Rodriguo scenes. A school play could be fun.

The auditions take place in the assembly hall through the lunch break. The head of English – mousy Mr Peterson – is supposed to be in charge, but its flamboyant Ms Kettering who's really running the show. She's our drama teacher, once an actress herself, with tight, corkscrew curls that cascade down her back and huge, red-rimmed glasses that she peers over.

She explains that all the girls who want to play Eliza will take turns getting up on the stage. There are fifteen of us, mostly from year nine and ten with a few, including me, from older year groups. At the last minute, the door opens and another girl bursts in. I stare in surprise.

It's Amy.

She never said a word about auditioning today. Her eyes widen as she spots me, clearly as surprised to see me here as I am to see her.

I press my fingers into my palm as I wait to be called. Ms Kettering wants each of us to read a poem or a few lines from a play. She's going to make a shortlist later today and have the finalists come back tomorrow to sing – a song of our choice – then she'll announce the parts on Friday.

I have no idea what I'll sing if I'm chosen.

My heart starts to thud.

"Let's start with you, Jo," Ms Kettering says with an encouraging smile. She knows me and is aware that I'm pretty confident, so she probably thinks I'm happy to go first. In fact I feel exposed. Stupid, even. Heart still thudding, I drag my suddenly too-heavy feet up the short flight of steps and on to the stage.

I peer out, across the empty space of the assembly hall. The other girls are looking up at me, but I don't meet their eyes. I fix my gaze on the clock on the wall at the other end of the room.

Ms Kettering clears her throat. "Ready when you are, Jo."

I take a deep breath. I can do this. I look down at the book in my hands, a collection of Shakespeare sonnets. "Let me not to the marriage of true minds. . ."

My voice steadies as I say the lines I've rehearsed – from a Shakespeare sonnet we've studied in class.

It's over at last. And from the impressed look of the girls in front of me, it didn't go too badly. Ms Kettering isn't giving anything away. She just thanks me, then turns to the first of the girls in year nine. "Go ahead, please."

As the girl reads something from her phone in a dull monotone, I look at Amy. Her gaze is fixed on the stage and her jaw is tight with tension. She's nervous, I realize with a jolt. My sense of relief vanishes and my nerves build again, this time for Amy.

The other girls deliver their lines. Some are good, a few are terrible. I am trying not to feel too cocky, but I think I was probably the best. Amy is left until last which must be as hard as having to go first. Not that you'd know it from the way she steps confidently up the stairs and into the centre of the stage.

My heart, which had only just stopped thudding, drums in my chest all over again. The room stills. The tension builds. I stare up at Amy, willing her to be all right. Which is when I realize that now she's on stage there is absolutely no sign of fear in her eyes. In fact, she's sweeping the room with her gaze, the very picture of confidence and already commanding more attention than everyone else put together. Any nerves she was feeling have clearly vanished. What's more, she isn't holding a book or piece of paper.

Does that mean she's going to speak her lines from memory?

There's a pause while Amy collects herself. Then she begins.

"Oh, Rodriguo," she cries, her voice shaking with emotion. She places one hand on her chest. "My heart is broken. I can feel the pieces fast falling under my trembling fingers."

My jaw drops. She's reciting Rachel, from my *own* story, from one of the scenes I made up over our Christmas holiday last year. Back then Amy was only allowed the tiniest of parts – Rachel's silent friend in the dormitory scenes or the school cat. Most of the time I made Meg play Rachel while I was Rodriguo. I watch Amy stride across the stage, her voice rising in the expressions of love for Rodriguo that Meg never delivered with half such emotion.

I'm astonished that Amy has remembered the words. Even more astonished at how good she is. As she finishes and walks off the stage, suddenly self-conscious, the others break into spontaneous applause. Ms Kettering is grinning from ear to ear.

It's so obvious Amy is the best. Clear she will get the part of Eliza.

A tumult of emotions tumble inside me. I'm furious she's used my ideas without asking, though hugely flattered that she chose to *and* that she remembered so many of the lines after all these months. And I'm jealous of her acting skills too, aware with biting clarity that she was way better than I was.

The applause subsides and Ms Kettering starts

talking about where and when she'll post the shortlist for the final audition tomorrow. Amy catches my eye, her expression part hope, part relief, part joy, part defiance. Beside her, a girl I don't know squeezes her arm and whispers something in her ear, but Amy is still looking at me.

And then pride surges through me, eclipsing all other feelings and, as Ms Kettering turns away, I rush over and swoop Amy into a big hug.

"You were brilliant," I whisper in her ear.

She pulls away, studying my face. "You didn't mind me using the Rodriguo thing?" she asks.

I hug her again. "Not at all," I say. "Though when you get to be a famous movie star, just remember how I gave you the words to launch your career."

"Whatevs." Amy pulls away again, laughing.

A bunch of the other girls swarm around her now and I slip away. Outside the air is crisp and cool. I message Meg to tell her what a great audition Amy just did.

Srsly amazing. WAY better than me. Guess I'll stick to writing stories – we all have our thing, don't we? I hesitate for a second, then add. *Glad you found yours. J x*

Meg replies with a row of hearts and kisses.

That night I write about the audition, adding it to

the story I've already made about Amy and how she's changed. About how *we* have changed.

I look back over the writing I've done over the last few weeks: one piece is about me and the ups and downs of my friendship with Lateef. Another describes Meg and her secret ambitions. And then there's my recent effort on Amy, who has always had a flair for the dramatic, one way or another. They're different from anything else I've written – and there is something about them that I really like. That I'm proud of. I just need to find a way of bringing them together into a single story that I can send to the editor, Marianne. This weekend, I decide, I will definitely make time to do that.

But when the weekend comes, something happens that makes me forget all about my writing. Something that changes everything, for ever.

Chapter 6

Saturday marks the start of October and our third weekend without Meg, though from the noise levels in the house you'd never know we were one sister down.

As predicted, Amy got the part of Eliza despite being one of the youngest girls to audition. She found out yesterday and is still on a high. Right now she and Katy Brown and their friends are playing some stupid game in the living room that involves an interactive video and a lot of shrieking.

Mum is playing music loudly – track after track of wailing folk music from way before even she was born – while she conducts one of her periodic decluttering sessions upstairs. Today she's focused on our wardrobes – especially all the stuff Meg has left behind and the racks of pink and frothy outfits Amy no longer wears. Neither of them will be happy when they see the bin bags Mum has filled with their clothes – which will mean a row – but right now Mum is lost in her own thoughts, an unhappy, far-away expression on her face as she wanders from room to room.

I guess she must miss Meg a lot.

I miss her too – though it *is* pretty cool having our room to myself. Meg and I are still messaging a lot – and it sounds like she's really happy at John Brooke. She's planning on coming home next weekend and I can't wait to see her.

Mum drifts in again, a turquoise dress dangling from her hands. "I found this in Amy's drawer. Is it Meg's? She was asking about a bluey-green dress on the phone yesterday, said she was sure she'd packed it. . ."

"That's Meg's – she'll be furious," I say with relish, but Mum just nods and wanders out again. I stare after her. Something is definitely up. Mum's hasn't really been herself for days. Neither has Dad.

I can't put my finger on what's wrong, but something is telling me it's more than missing Meg.

Mum's music is still blaring out, so I retreat to the bathroom where I sit propped against the bath, with my laptop balanced on my knees. It's quieter in here, although I now face regular interruptions from Amy's friends who keep creeping in to reapply their lip gloss and eyeliner.

Outside the sun emerges from behind a cloud. It's been chillier the past few days but looking through the window I can see Dad has taken off his jumper and is staring at a rose bush with his shirtsleeves rolled up. He wipes his eyes with the back of his hand.

Is he crying?

Feeling really uneasy, I watch as he strolls out of sight. A few moments later the front door opens, then shuts again.

I'm too distracted to write any more, so I pick up the brush by the sink and run it through my hair, watching how the static lifts the individual chestnut brown strands.

Amy appears at the bathroom door. "I need to pee," she announces.

"Who was at the front door?" I ask.

"No one, it was Dad going out," Amy says.

"Where?"

Amy shrugs. "He said he needed crumpets or something for the garden."

I frown. "Crumpets? That doesn't—"

"What's Mum doing?" Amy asks.

"Clearing out old clothes. By the way. . ." I fold my arms, summoning my sternest expression. "You're totally busted on that turquoise dress of Meg's. . ."

Amy makes a face. At least Amy is her usual self. I leave her in the bathroom and, laptop under my arm, I head downstairs, musing on my story for Teen Spiral and how I can find a way of tying my three separate pieces of writing together.

Beth is reading at the kitchen table.

"Hey," she says smiling up at me. "You OK?"

"Fine," I say, "though Mum and Dad seem . . . I dunno, like something's not right."

Beth nods, the smile slipping from her face. There are dark rings under her eyes.

"Are *you* OK, Beth?"

"I'm fine," she says, but there's hesitation in her voice.

"Beth?" I persist. "What's going on?"

"Tea?" Beth asks, ignoring me.

"Sure." I sit down at the table. I'm still determined to find out what is wrong, but there's no point me pushing her. I know my Beth. She will tell me when she's ready, I just have to be patient.

Beth turns to the kettle and fills it with water.

"By the way," I say. "Why is Dad buying crumpets for the garden?"

"He isn't, he's getting *compost*," Beth explains. "Why did you—?"

"Amy," I say.

"Ah." Beth flicks the kettle on to boil and sits down opposite me. "How's your story coming?" she asks.

"Actually, I'm stuck," I say, laying my laptop on the table between us.

"Mmm," Beth says. "What's the problem?"

"I've got three different pieces," I say. "They're all good, I think, but there's something not quite working. It's like they're . . . bitty and I want to connect them and I can't see how."

"So there's a missing link?" Beth asks.

"Exactly."

The kettle boils and Beth fetches teabags and two mugs. I reach around to take the milk out of the fridge. "I really want what I'm writing to work for Teen Spiral."

"What matters is that it works for *you*," Beth says, filling our mugs with water.

"I guess." I smile at her. There's something about Beth that calms me, soothes me. It always has. I am filled with affection for her. She still looks so tired, with those shadows under her eyes. I hate that she's stuck in the house so much. She says she doesn't mind missing school, but it must be lonely. Maybe if she got out and about a bit more, she would feel better.

I add a big splash of milk to Beth's mug – she likes her tea milky – and a smaller dash to my own.

"We should get you out and about," I say cheerfully. "Go and do something active together. What about that zip wire Lateef mentioned last week? The new one in Ringstone Wood – it's supposed to be the third highest in the country. We could all go and watch Amy shrieking all the way down."

Beth laughs. "That sounds like fun for *you*, Jo; I'd just be terrified for her. And definitely for myself."

"If you don't want to risk the zip wire you could just wrap up warm and watch the rest of us." I grimace. "Though that doesn't sound like much fun."

"Wrapping up warm and watching sounds perfect," Beth says.

"Oh come on, Bethy," I urge. "You've got to take a few risks, you know? Now you're getting better you need to push yourself a bit."

She looks at me and, to my horror, tears well in her dark eyes.

"*No.* Beth, *what?* Did I put my foot in it?" I fill up with remorse. "I'm sorry, I didn't mean to upset you. Oh, I *knew* something was wrong."

Beth cups her mug of tea. The silence in the kitchen somehow seems louder than all the noises around us. A tear trickles down her cheek.

"Beth?" A weight settles on my chest. I've been patient, waiting for her to speak, but I can't wait any longer. "*Beth? Please.*"

Beth meets my gaze squarely. "Jo," she says. "I made Mum and Dad promise not to say, because I wanted to tell you this myself." She takes a deep breath. "We saw the doctor this week and they confirmed the tests I've been having. I've . . . I've got cancer."

The kitchen spins around us. I look deep into Beth's eyes.

No. Not Beth. This can't be true.

"Are they . . . sure?" I ask, my voice faltering. But even as I speak I know it's true. It explains why she's stayed off school. All those doctor's appointments. It explains how haggard Dad looks, how preoccupied Mum has been, how sad and distracted they've both seemed.

Beth nods. "It's a kind of lymphoma, early stage

and treatable, but. . ." She hesitates. "It's not connected to me being ill earlier in the year, but Mum and Dad are still beating themselves up for spending so much time away from home." She meets my gaze. "You have to help me look after them, Jo. They're so upset."

My heart flips in my chest. This is pure Beth, worrying about everyone else, not thinking of herself.

"What about you?" The words rasp out of me. I take her hand, lying pale on the table. She feels cold. "Beth? How are you feeling?"

She shrugs. "I don't know," she says in a soft voice. "I've got to have chemotherapy, other stuff too."

I squeeze her hand, no idea what to say. The world has just tipped on its axis, spinning off in a different direction. Changed, for ever.

"You can always tell me how you feel," I say, my voice breaking. "I'm not going to pretend I won't get upset, but it won't be like talking to Mum and Dad." I straighten my back. I have to be strong, I realize, not just for Beth but for all of them. "If you're scared, you can tell me."

Beth nods. "Thanks, Jo. I don't want Meg to know until I can tell her in person, when she comes home next weekend. Mum and Dad think it's better if we wait and tell Amy then too. OK?"

"OK," I say, feeling numb.

"Thanks, Jo." She sits back, taking her hand out of mine.

A moment passes. "Are . . . are you scared?" The words feel like they squeeze out of me.

"Only for all of you." Beth smiles.

We sit in silence for a few more moments. A loud burst of laughter from Amy next door rises up then subsides into chatter.

"I'm glad you know," Beth says.

And then she turns her head to gaze out at the garden.

Chapter 7

Lateef sits beside me, his face uncharacteristically solemn.

"Are you sure about this, Jo?" he asks.

I nod, looking into the mirror that runs along the wall in front of us.

"Do you want me to stay?" Lateef adds.

"No, I'll do it alone," I say, meeting his eyes.

"Right," Lateef says, standing up. He goes to the bathroom door and curls his fingers around the handle. He hesitates for a second, then turns back, looking at my reflection. "You're the most extraordinary person I've ever met, Jo March," he says very quietly.

Then he turns and leaves me sitting in front of the mirror.

It's the beginning of December, two months since Beth told me how sick she was. Meg and Amy found out soon after, on Meg's first visit home. Neither of them reacted how I expected. Meg, who is always so practical, burst into tears and started saying that she was going to leave John Brooke College and come home and never go away again. Dad told her sternly she was to do no such thing, though of course she could come back every weekend if she wanted.

Amy was the opposite. Little Miss Emotional Outburst was, for once, business-like and practical. Asking exactly what was wrong with Beth, and what her treatments would involve. Mum and Dad answered her questions as best they could.

At the time I don't think any of us really understood.

We do now.

Beth's been having chemotherapy treatment for weeks. Mum takes her to the special cancer centre at the hospital every Tuesday. When Beth comes back she's exhausted, and though she usually feels a bit better by the weekend, the following Tuesday the whole cycle begins again. She hasn't complained about anything except once, earlier this week, when I found her crying in this very bathroom.

"What is it?" I asked, taking her hand.

Beth looked up at her reflection. Her sweet face all blotchy and her eyes red-rimmed.

"It's my *hair*," she sobbed.

She'd been nearly bald for a while, just a few soft fuzzy strands remaining, and that afternoon she'd asked Mum to shave off the rest. Since then she's been wearing little caps and insisting she really likes how cosy they make her head feel.

But I know the truth.

"You don't have to pretend Beth," I told her. "It's OK to tell us how hard it is."

"Oh, Jo," she said back, her voice barely a whisper. "I feel so stupid about being upset. It's just hair."

"I know." I hugged her. "But you're not stupid."

"It's not that I mind losing the hair," she said, swallowing down her sobs. "It's . . . it's. . ."

"It's that you hate being different. Standing out," I said. "I know."

And now you won't have to.

I stare at myself in the mirror.

It's time.

Half an hour later and I leave the bathroom. Upstairs is empty. They are all downstairs in the kitchen: my parents and my three sisters. Mum has called me twice for tea. I've got to face them. Show them what I've done.

I don't regret it but, as I make my way down the stairs, I wish I didn't have to face them all together. Still, there's no other choice now.

The air feels cool on the back of my neck. I reach the kitchen door and peer round. Everyone is in their seat – Mum and Dad at either end of the table. Meg and Amy opposite the door, Beth with her back to me, next to my own empty seat.

As I walk across the kitchen, my heart in my mouth, Mum looks up.

Her jaw drops.

"Oh, Jo," Dad says, his voice a mix of shock and awe. "Oh, my Jo."

I glance at Meg and Amy. They're both staring at my head.

My bald, shaved head.

I brace myself, expecting one or both of them to laugh. But they don't. Amy's eyes fill with tears. Meg gives me a slight, reassuring nod.

Beth is the slowest to move, turning in her chair. And then she sees me and gasps.

Her hand flies to her little pink cap. Our eyes meet.

For a split second I'm terrified that she's going to hate me for what I've done. I mean, what am I trying to say? That I'm sharing Beth's experience? Of course I'm not. She's coping with cancer and chemo.

I've just got to face a few months without hair.

The silence swells and fills the room. I want to say something meaningful, but I don't, for once, have any words.

"Jo?" Beth takes off her cap. Her scalp shines pink under the kitchen light.

I shrug. "Couldn't let you have all the fun, could I?"

"But your beautiful hair," Beth's voice is barely a breath.

"Actually it suits you, Jo," Amy says thoughtfully. "You kind of rock it, in fact."

Meg nods. "You do," she says, her voice filling with warmth and wonder.

Dad clears his throat.

Mum stands up. She comes over and takes my

hands. "*I* think you've never looked more beautiful in your life, Jo."

She looks me deep in the eyes, an expression overflowing with love and pride.

"Now sit down before your tea gets cold."

"Not to mention your head," Meg adds.

And, with a smile, I take my place next to Beth, surrounded by my family.

Chapter 8

It's the week before Christmas and the house is empty. It's hard to believe that a year ago I sat in this same living room with my sisters, complaining about our lack of presents.

Right now all I can think about is Beth.

I wander from room to room, the silence weighing down on me. How many times in the past year did I wish for this kind of peace and quiet? And now I have it, how heavy it feels, like a dead weight.

For the past month there's only been one story I wanted to tell, and I finished it last week. It's about Beth – a record of her illness and her courage, with elements from the three other pieces I'd written, about the rest of us, her sisters, woven in.

I realized, you see, that Beth's story was what was missing.

My Beth. The missing link.

Because Beth might be quiet and shy and easy for most people to overlook, but without her at the heart of our family, we don't work.

Marianne at Teen Spiral loves what I wrote. She called and told me so yesterday, said that *My Beth* is exactly the kind of thing she was looking for. "It feels real and honest," she said. "Exactly what we want for the big launch."

I was ... I am ...thrilled. But I've got life in perspective now. Some things are more important than even a story.

I glance at the time. Mum and Dad are at a hospital appointment with Beth. Her chemotherapy treatments are over – for now at least – and today they find out how effective this first stage has been. I can't do anything until I know if she's OK.

I go upstairs to my room, look at my piles of schoolwork and then at the pictures above my bed. The oldest photos, of Notre Dame and the Grand Canyon and the Taj Mahal, are yellowing at the edges. One day I will leave home for good, earn enough money to travel around the world then go to uni and work in London to fund my writing until I can live off my books. At least that's what I hope.

I sit on the bed. Strange, how much I can look forward to the future and how much I fear it too. Weird, how many times I've longed to be alone in the house and, now that I am, how a part of me can't wait for everyone to come home.

A knock at the front door breaks into my daydreaming.

Lateef is on the doorstep. He's holding a small fir tree on a stand and smiling. He's been amazing these past few months, distracting me, dragging me out, sending me jokes and links to new songs he thinks I'll love. We don't talk about Beth much, but every now and then he'll give me a look that says he's here for me. My best friend.

"Uncle Jim sent me over with this. He thought you might not have had time to get a tree."

"Oh, that's kind of him." I'm hugely touched – we never even thought of getting a tree. But then gruff Uncle Jim *is* kind. I stand back to let Lateef through. He takes the tree into the living room, where a cardboard box I hadn't noticed before stands in front of the TV. It has XMAS DECS in Mum's neat, round handwriting on the side.

Lateef sets up the tree by the fire.

"Should we decorate it?" he asks.

"Sure," I say, then, "No. Let's wait till Beth gets back."

Our eyes meet.

"When will they be home?" Lateef asks. He knows all about this hospital appointment – and how much it means to all of us.

"Soon."

Lateef opens his mouth as if he's about to speak, but before he can say anything the front door slams open and Amy and Meg clatter into the house, Meg insisted they went out earlier to a pop-up fashion show in Ringstone. She said she thought it would be good for them to get out of the house for a bit.

". . .the dress was *magenta*," Amy insists.

"It was *crimson*," Meg says, exasperated.

Lateef grins as the pair of them walk into the living room.

"Lateef!" Amy says. I think I see her cheeks flush, or maybe they were already pink thanks to the chilly air outside. The tip of her nose is definitely red from the cold. She is wearing a bobble hat over her sleek hair and a thick scarf, above which her eyes sparkle. She looks, I realize with a jolt, properly beautiful. She's still just a teenager, but there's no trace of the little girl who moved here a year ago.

"Nice tree." Meg nods approvingly at the little fir as she takes off her gloves. She has changed too, in the last year. She's grown up somehow, like she's more sure of who she is: very happy at college but carrying responsibilities that weigh her down too. She doesn't mention Beth directly, but worry is etched on her face, as I know it is on mine.

"It's the best one from the garden," Lateef explains.

"Beth'll love decorating it," I add. "And if she doesn't have the energy to do it herself, she can tell us where she wants the baubles or whatever to go."

Meg nods. She glances at me, eyebrows raised. I know what she's asking.

"No news," I say, "but they should be back any minute."

A heavy silence hangs over the room.

"Hey, Amy," Lateef says, and there's something strangely tentative in his voice that makes me glance at him. "Have I told you that you were great as Eliza in *My Fair Lady*?"

"Only a million times," I say, rolling my eyes.

"Thanks, I *adored* doing it." Amy blushes, more deeply than before.

"*That's* magenta," Meg says, pointing at Amy's cheeks.

As we all laugh, a key turns in the front door. A gust of cold air is followed by Dad's heavy tread. Lighter footsteps follow in his wake. The four of us in the living room fall silent. I hold my breath, waiting, both wanting and dreading them coming in. Part of me is desperate to know if Beth's going to be all right. But part of me would rather wait, put the moment off – in case the news is bad.

"I'll put the kettle on," I hear Dad saying.

"Bed or sofa downstairs?" Mum asks. She sounds cheerful, but then she always does, even when things are bad.

"Downstairs, definitely," Beth says.

A second later she appears in the living-room door. Her eyes fall on the tree.

"Oh," she says, clasping her hands together. "That's so pretty."

"How was it?" I ask.

The room throbs with the tension. Mum appears behind Beth. She's smiling. Is that a good sign? Or a brave face?

"Mum?" Meg asks.

"Mum?" I echo, unable to bear it any longer. "What *happened*?"

She lays a hand on Beth's shoulder. "I'll let Beth tell you," she says quietly.

Beth looks at us, smiling shyly. "The doctors say that they managed to catch the cancer at such an early stage that it's gone into remission. I've still got to have more treatments but it's good news." She smiles again, a proper smile this time. "Really good news."

There's a moment of silence, then joy washes over me like a wave and I jump up, laughing and cheering and crying. Meg and Amy are too, the three of us hugging each other and Mum and Beth – and then, when Dad appears, all of us hurl ourselves at him.

At last peace descends and Mum and Dad retreat to the kitchen to make tea.

I'm still beaming at Beth, though Meg and Amy have sat down again. She runs her hand through her hair which is covered with a light brown fuzz.

"It's starting to grow back." She points at my scalp. "For you, too."

I nod, my heart too full to speak. It hits me that this right here, right now, is what really matters: us, together, no matter how far our lives take us from where we started and whatever we find when we get there. I slip my arm around Beth and pull Meg and Amy towards me too. My sisters.

"Should I go?" Lateef asks, suddenly uncertain.

"Definitely not," Beth says firmly. "You're family too."

I gulp down the lump in my throat. "You don't get out of helping to decorate our tree that easily," I poke him in the ribs, then turn to the tree, still propped up against the wall by the fireplace.

"We can't leave it there," Meg exclaims. "It's too close to the gas fire."

"It'll look much better by the window," Amy insists.

"Except then you won't be able to get past it to reach the curtains," I point out.

"How about moving it to the other side of the fireplace, nearer to the door?" Beth suggests.

"It'll lose all visual impact," Amy argues.

I roll my eyes. "Why don't we put it right in the middle of the room, then?"

"And have us all trip over it every time we come in and out?" Meg says.

Beth laughs. "Lateef, why don't you choose?"

Lateef looks alarmed. "Er, thanks but no. I'm not

getting involved in a March girls argument. Just let me know when you've decided."

And Beth laughs again as Meg, Amy and I all speak at once, our voices rising into the warm air, filling the house with the sound of home.

The timeless story of ***Little Women*** is also available
in our new classics range...

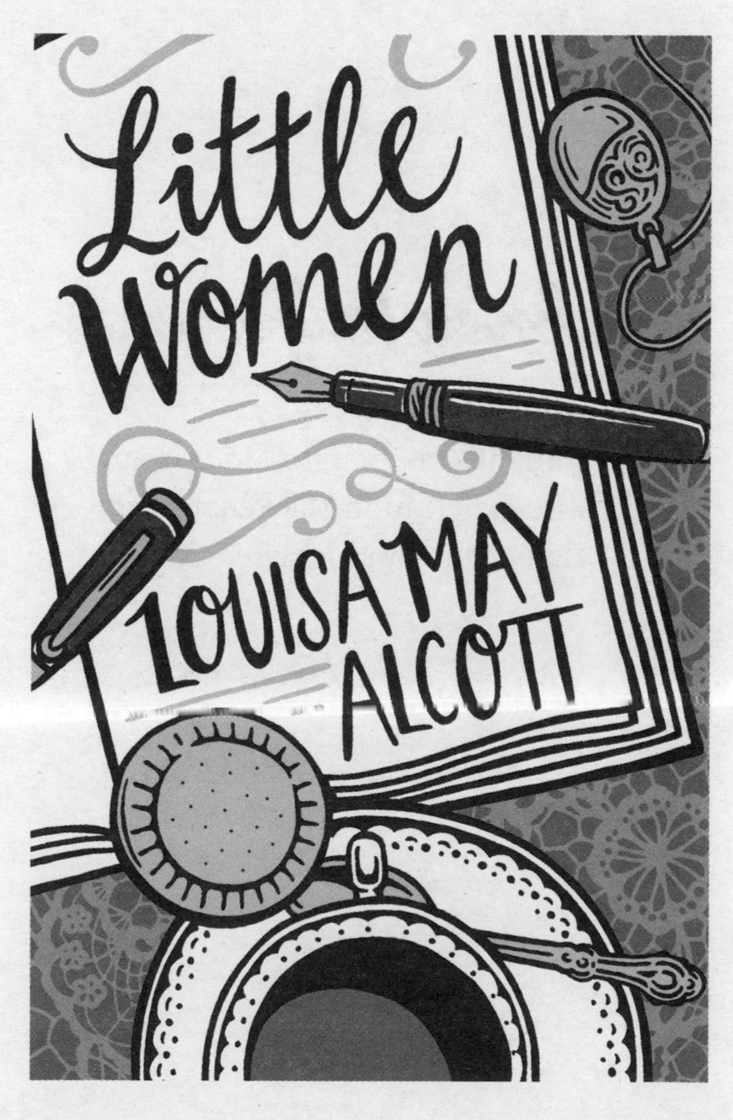

Acknowledgements

With thanks, as ever, to Moira Young, Lou Kuenzler, Julie Mackenzie, Gaby Halberstam and Melanie Edge.